The Mystery of Green Hill

by Ivan Kušan

(available in hard-cover editions)

THE MYSTERY OF GREEN HILL

KOKO AND THE GHOSTS

The
Mystery of Green Hill

Ivan Kušan

Translated from the Serbo-Croat by Michael B. Petrovich
Illustrated by Kermit Adler

A VOYAGER BOOK
HARCOURT, BRACE & WORLD, INC.
New York

ISBN 0-15-663972-6

English translation © 1962 by Harcourt, Brace & World, Inc.

All rights reserved. No part of this publication may
be reproduced or utilized in any form or by any means,
electronic or mechanical, including photocopy, recording,
or any information storage and retrieval system,
without permission in writing from the publisher.

Originally published in Yugoslavia by Matica Hrvatska, Zagreb,
under the title of
UZBUNA NA ZELENOM VRHU
B.2.70
Library of Congress Catalog Card Number: 62-8743
Printed in the United States of America

Contents

The Characters in This Story

KOKO (real name Ratko) MILICH, twelve years old, has just finished the sixth grade. A boy whose hair always needs combing and whose nose ends in a point. He has the bad habit of scratching himself behind the ear.

MARY, his black-haired sister, nine years old, about to enter the fourth grade.

BOZO TUCICH, eleven years old. A dreamy, rather puny boy. Even though he is young, he has already completed the sixth grade. He wears glasses and sees better at night than in the daytime.

COCKROACH (real name Vincent) LEIB, fourteen years old. He has completed junior high school. A tall, strong boy with black hair and large, remarkably green eyes. Overly given to reading comic books.

TOM BRAN, twelve years old, has completed the sixth grade. A scrawny, shy lad.

IVO BRAN, eighteen years old. The hair on his upper lip is already beginning to grow, which is probably why he thinks that he can smoke.

BLACKY, fifteen years old. Has completed only elementary school. A black-haired boy, the tallest and thinnest of all the boys. Overly fond of spitting left and right.

EMMIE RADICH, eleven years old, has finished the fifth grade. A lovely blond girl with big brown eyes.

PARENTS AND RELATIVES: There are many of them and not all appear in this story. Some of the boys no longer have fathers, but all have mothers. Cockroach has a sister, Blacky has a baby brother, and Emmie an aunt, but none of these is important here.

ISAAC, an old woodcutter with a long white beard. He lives in a rickety shack on the edge of the forest.

MARIO, a queer would-be poet. His only friend is a gray tomcat.

LUCY BOBICH, a lonely widow.

THE TONCHICHES, an elderly couple.

The Mystery of Green Hill

1

Danger

"Don't cry, Mary, we'll buy another dog, bigger and nicer looking than Gypsy was," said Koko, scratching himself behind the ear with his left hand and not daring to look either at his sister or at the body of the black dog.

"I don't wa-a-ant another dog, I want Gypsy, m-y-y Gypsy," Mary sobbed, while her shoulders bobbed up and down like a boat on the waves. "I want my own Gypsy . . ." She stroked the dark fur of the motionless body that lay in the shade of a little peach tree.

Gypsy had been a favorite of the whole house, but it was nine-year-old Mary who loved him the most. Her brother, who was now standing over her, tried to hide his sorrow, for he knew that it was not right for him to cry, even over a dead dog. In the fall he would be going into the seventh grade. Even so, while his sister was leaning over, he quickly brushed away a tear that was caught on his eyelash.

"Why . . . why did they poison him? Tell me, Koko, why?" Mary asked in a trembling voice.

"You know why . . . so they could steal our chickens. Some very bad men must have done it."

That morning the Milich household had been in a real uproar. When Mary's father got up at dawn, he went into the yard, as he did every morning, to wash himself under the cold stream of water from the pump. But the green pump with its big curved handle was no longer there. All that was left was a long pipe that stuck out of the grass like an exclamation point. Then his eyes fell on the battered-down door of the chicken house, inside which there was no longer a single chicken, not even the big, saucy rooster. He whistled for Gypsy, but Gypsy did not answer. He could not, for he was lying lifeless under the little tree. On his jaws could be seen some green foam. Milich called his wife, and she began to cry. There would be no more eggs or roast chicken on Sundays. And the water pump had been very expensive. They would have to save a long time to get a new one. Of course, she was also sad over Gypsy.

Koko woke up and knew at once that something terrible had happened. Otherwise, his mother would not be crying. She had cried only once before. That was two years ago, when she received the news that their father had been wounded in battle. He quickly jumped out of bed and ran into the yard barefooted.

His father was just about to leave for work and was trying to comfort his mother.

"That's that! There's nothing that anyone can do about it. I shall work evenings. In two or three months we'll have everything as before. Conditions will get better, and this sort of thing will not happen again. Why, the war only ended some twenty days ago. Only don't forget to go to the police. It doesn't concern only us. There's no point in others losing something too."

Mrs. Milich, whose eyes were still red from weeping, nodded her head. She would be sure to go. "There is no doubt that this is the work of a gang. The night before, the same thing happened at Lucy's. Oh, why weren't we more careful . . . ?"

So it was that Koko learned they had been visited by thieves during the night. After such exciting news, he could not go back to bed, but he was sorry it was so early—not yet six o'clock—and that he could not tell his friends the unusual news. "Real robbers," he thought. "Real robbers, with knives and guns, here in our garden, in our yard. Maybe they looked through the window, maybe they were watching me. If I had moved, if I had moved only a little bit, they certainly would have stabbed me."

He almost forgot, for a moment, that their beautiful pump was no longer there and the fine rooster with his crooked beak and huge waving crest. But then he remembered Gypsy. The dog had been Koko's pride and had made him especially happy because no one dared to enter the yard while Gypsy lunged against his chain and growled threateningly. They had to call Koko, who would then quiet the dog with a wave of his hand. Even his friend Cockroach, brave and big though he was, did not dare to enter—and he was not afraid of anything, not of the graveyard or even old Isaac, who lived at the edge of the nearby forest.

When Koko's sister Mary got up and when they had carefully told her that Gypsy was no more, his throat tightened up and he kept repeating to himself, "I will not, I will not, I will not cry. I am too big for that." Just to comfort his sister, he said that they would get a new dog, and then suddenly he realized that this was really possible. Their father would work evenings, and in two or three months they might have another black dog whom only he, Koko, would dare pet.

"Yes, he will be bigger, much, much bigger, and the tip of his tail will be all white. Come on, Sis, let's bury old Gypsy. You know, he would have died of old age anyway."

"He would not . . . he would not. Gypsy was still young. He was born when I was, and teacher told us that dogs live a long time. Gypsy would have lived as long as I, maybe even longer. . . ."

"Come on, Mary! We'll bury him in the garden, under the tallest apple tree, near the fence."

"All right, I will carry him. . . ."

But Gypsy was too heavy. Koko had to carry him, while Mary followed, holding on to Gypsy's long tail. Their mother came to the door, turned her head aside so as not to look at the sad sight, and called, "Ratko, hurry up if you want to go to town with me."

Koko was not pleased to be called by his real name, for he did not like it. But his parents did not wish to call him by the nickname his friends had given him. He frowned a bit. For the last two days he had been happily looking forward to going to town. He had heard that there were many soldiers there dressed in new uniforms and carrying shiny, polished weapons. Cockroach even claimed that he had seen guns with cartridge belts that contained a thousand bullets and that fired without stopping.

"We'll hurry," he called back, taking hold of the spade, which was leaning against the wall. "In ten minutes."

The ground under the big apple tree was hard. And every once in a while Koko's foot slipped off the spade. The sun had now risen, and Koko was already in a good sweat. Mary fetched an old torn tablecloth in which she wrapped the dead dog.

"I will write his name and the date on a board, and we will stick it into the ground above Gypsy's head. All right?" Koko asked, wiping the sweat from his forehead.

"Fine. But shouldn't we set up a cross?"

"No, not a cross. He wasn't baptized." Her brother smiled. "We'll give him a nice board, and I will . . ."

"Why wasn't he baptized? If we gave him a name, we must have baptized him."

"I know . . . we did, but anyway. . . . Oh, don't bother me. I'll set up a board and I'll write . . ."

"No you won't. . . . I'll write the name and the date and the year and everything. I know how to write and"—Mary hesitated a bit—"I liked him more."

"But he liked me more," Koko asserted, measuring the depth of the hole with the handle of the spade.

"He did not, he did not. . . . He liked me more. . . .

Whenever I came home from school . . . and anyway . . . and always . . ."

"But I fed him . . . and he always came to me, while he didn't even notice you. . . ."

"He did, he did. You're jealous!" Mary clenched her fists, shook her head, and stamped her foot on the mound of dug-up earth. "Give me the spade. I'll bury Gypsy myself. Come on . . . let me-e-e. Ma-a-a-ma, look at him. . . ."

"What's the matter now? Quarreling again? As though I didn't have enough to worry about, without having trouble with you. Hurry up if you want to go, and don't tease Mary."

"I . . ." Koko started to say, but he remembered that he might lose out on the visit to town, and so he decided not to reply. He let go of the spade without even looking at the hole he had dug or at his angry sister, and he thought to himself, "I will get me a big gray dog. And he won't be called Gypsy but Sultan. Yes, Sultan. And nobody will be allowed to touch him. He will listen just to me." Then he stopped, thought a bit, scratched himself behind the left ear, and added, "He will be called King. That is a nicer name for a dog."

Before he went back into the house, Koko spied his neighbor Bozo peering over the fence. He had to tell him the news at once, for they probably would not see one another again until that afternoon. He glanced quickly toward the house to see where his mother was, whistled, and ran to the fence that separated their large yard from Bozo's little house. Bozo was a frail boy, a year younger than Koko, with a big head and narrow shoulders, bushy eyebrows, and a dreamy, shortsighted look. Everyone admired his ability and intelligence, but still everyone was glad that he was not like Bozo. Thanks to Koko's whistle and his strange behavior, Bozo knew that something unusual and serious had happened. As soon as Koko reached the fence, Bozo whispered softly, "What is it? What's the matter?"

"Robbers!" hissed Koko, looking around as though afraid that someone was after him.

"What robbers? Where?" Bozo was stunned. His blue eyes, showing through his misty glasses, were opened wide in amazement.

"They were at our place last night. They stole the chickens, killed Gypsy, took away the pump . . ."

"How come nobody heard them?"

Koko was surprised by this reasonable question. Indeed, how was it that no one at all had heard anything?

"They were careful . . . I mean . . ." Koko suddenly looked around again and then lowered his voice. "I mean I did wake up, only don't tell anybody, for Father would be angry if he found out. I woke up and saw one of them, with a handkerchief across his nose and mouth, next to my window. I didn't dare move. Something was shining in his hand. A knife or a gun. If I had had a gun or something on me . . ."

"No, it's good that you didn't do anything," said Bozo, and lowered his head as though he were thinking it over. "What are you going to do now?"

"Mother and I are going to town. We're going to the police. They will certainly catch the thieves."

"I'm going to tell the other kids. Will they be surprised! Maybe they've gone swimming already."

Koko was almost sorry for having blurted out everything to Bozo, for he wanted to tell the gang himself about the terrible events of the night before. It occurred to him that it might be good to add that even in his sleep he had heard Gypsy softly whining. However, his mother was apt to call him again at any moment, and so he decided to postpone a more detailed description for later.

"Sure," he said hurriedly, "tell them that I'll be back

about noon and that I'll tell them all about it. By then I'll know what the police are going to do. O.K., so long."

Both boys hurried off. Bozo went carefully and looked where he was going. Koko ran as fast as he could. From the house came his mother's impatient voice:

"Ratko-o-o! Ratko-o-o!"

2

Secret Council at the Water's Edge

Bozo had guessed that his friends were already at the little lake, west of the village of Green Hill, which was surrounded by a thick forest on three sides. He was not wrong. On the other side of the lake, below a concrete pillbox that stood at the foot of a hill, he could see Cockroach, Blacky, and Tom. They stood close together, as though they were examining something very carefully. Bozo wanted to tell them the unusual news as soon as possible, so he began to run around the lake. He was the only one among them who did not know how to swim, or else he might have swum across now.

"Look," said Tom, gazing in the direction of the forest. "Bozo's coming."

"And he's running too," observed Blacky, a tall, lean boy of fifteen who was older than the rest and knew it too. "Will you look at that! How could he see that we have a bicycle here!"

"Maybe he got himself a new pair of stronger glasses," Cockroach suggested, and began to laugh, leaning on the big blue bicycle whose handles he was holding with both hands.

As Bozo ran up to them, he finally saw the bicycle, which Cockroach's father had only yesterday taken down from the attic where it had lain hidden throughout the war.

"What's the matter? What are you puffing for?" asked Tom.

"Do you want to try to ride it?" Cockroach inquired,

ready to burst into laughter again. "Maybe you'll find it easier than swimming."

Everyone laughed. Even Bozo's eyes crinkled up at the corners. Meanwhile, he examined the wonderful two-wheeled bike. It was really something—no doubt about it—only he would never dare get up on it.

"No, I don't want to ride," he said seriously, as though they had really offered him a ride. "That's not important now."

"And what is important then, old man?" said Blacky gaily, winking at his friends.

"The important thing now is—robbers."

The three looked at one another. This answer was interesting, but they could not understand it.

"Well," Cockroach exclaimed, "what d'you know! What kind of robbers are you talking about?"

"Maybe they took your gold away!" said Blacky. Then he suddenly grew serious, for he remembered that they had decided not to make fun of Bozo's poverty. To correct his error, he placed a friendly hand on Bozo's shoulder and added, "Come on, please, tell us. What has happened?"

"The night before last they robbed Lucy. Last night they visited the Miliches. They took away all their chickens and their pump. And they poisoned Gypsy."

"What?" Cockroach suddenly shouted and laid the bicycle carefully on the ground. "This morning my dog Viking died. Mother almost cried. What if . . . ?"

For a moment they fell silent, and then Tom spoke up.

"Who could have done it? Who are the robbers?"

They looked at him pityingly.

"That's just the point. We don't know who did it, jughead," Blacky snapped, and spat through his teeth at a yellow butterfly resting on a wide blade of grass. "Why are we always saying *they, they?* Maybe only one man did it by himself."

"No, there were at least two of them," Bozo declared, wiping his glasses against the sleeve of his shirt. "Koko saw them."

"Go on!" Cockroach shouted again. "Saw them?"

"Who?" Tom asked.

"Then why didn't he yell for someone? Why didn't he throw something at them? Why didn't he at least call for help?"

"Well, if you'd just let me finish," Bozo said importantly, pushing up his newly cleaned glasses on his hooked nose. He knew that at this moment he was the most interesting fellow in the whole crowd, and he tried to take advantage of an opportunity he did not often have. "Koko told me everything: he suddenly woke up during the night, for he heard some strange sounds even through his sleep. It was a clear, completely clear night, and the stars . . ."

"Hey, you're off the track again, my poetic friend," Cockroach grumbled, coming closer to the storyteller as though threatening him.

"No descriptions, please," Blacky reminded him as he also took a step forward.

"Faster," urged the third listener. "Faster."

"All right, listen. Well, Koko woke up and recognized from the sound that it was Gypsy whining."

"Cramps!" said Cockroach knowingly. "Go on."

"As soon as he heard Gypsy, he knew that something was wrong. Then he heard the flutter of wings and the cackling of that big rooster of theirs. That's the same rooster who . . ."

"Faster," Tom urged.

"Oh, yes. And then he heard footsteps and wanted to call for help, because he had no . . . no weapons around. He had nothing on him. But, just at that moment, at that very moment when he wanted to shout, the worst thing of all happened!"

"What? What happened?" the three asked all at once.

"His bed is next to the window. And he no sooner moved and opened his mouth than something flashed before his eyes: it was a knife. The robber was standing beside the window. Over his mouth and nose he had a green handkerchief, and only his shining eyes could be seen. Koko shut his eyes. A little later he heard someone whistling softly at the gate, and then the masked man disappeared. . . ."

"You're lying!" said Blacky. "You made it all up!"

"Oh, there you go again. So I made it all up. Koko will tell you all about it when he comes back."

"And where is he?" Tom asked.

"Yeah, where is Koko?"

"He went with his mother to the police to report the robbery. Later he'll come here, and then you can ask him whether all this is the truth or not," the storyteller with the glasses concluded somberly, as though he himself believed that everything had happened in just that way.

"O.K., I believe you. Only one thing is a lie: that part about the handkerchief," Cockroach broke in, bending down and lifting the bicycle. "Everybody knows that in such cases robbers wear *black* handkerchiefs. It just seemed green to Koko in the dark."

"Because he was afraid," Blacky added.

Bozo stared blankly in front of him. He was thinking of everything that had disappeared: Gypsy, the pump, the rooster, Viking. Couldn't something be done? Was there nothing they could do? His head was buzzing with all sorts of ideas, and he himself was surprised when he suddenly spoke up.

"Anyway"—he carelessly dug at the soft ground with his shoe—"couldn't we do something?"

"Something?" two of the boys asked at the same time.

"Yeah . . . something . . . about the robbers."

"We?" Blacky laughed. "The police will have it all taken care of in two days."

Cockroach said nothing. Only his eyes began to sparkle. He was probably thinking that they *could* do something, but he did not want to speak too soon, so he kept quiet.

"Well," Bozo spoke again, "let's wait for Koko to come back."

"Yes, that's right," Cockroach added. "Meanwhile, I move that we adjourn to the vineyard behind the forest. Let's make the most of it until the watchman comes back."

"I second the motion," said Blacky. "Enough of all this crazy talk about robbers."

"Let's go," Bozo agreed.

Only Tom had said nothing, he was so amazed. Silently he traipsed after his friends, who were already beyond the pill-box.

3

"Don't Get Us Wrong"

Koko was disappointed with the town. One could hardly tell that the war was over and that peace had come. Everywhere the streets were littered with heaps of bricks, tiles, shattered glass, empty shells, and battered helmets. There were not many soldiers to be seen, and those he passed did not have new uniforms, though they were carrying the mysterious guns that fired without stopping. Here and there, there were big gashes in the earth made by bombs and mines. The movie theaters were not yet opened, nor were most of the stores.

"Mama, has peace really come? When will we have white bread to eat? In peacetime we had white bread, didn't we?"

"Ah, my son. Be patient a bit. Everything has been destroyed, burned down, demolished. Nobody in the country has had time to worry about the harvest. What little harvest there was the enemy has taken away."

Mrs. Milich sighed deeply and looked at the basket she had brought with her in the hope that she might buy something in the big market. All it contained was a bunch of carrots and two heads of cabbage. "It is fortunate," she thought, "that we have our small orchard and garden."

She took big strides, and her son could barely keep up with her as he hopped along, constantly turning about to look at things as they went. The streetcars were not yet in operation. The power lines lay on the streets like the torn webs of enormous spiders. Before long, they came to the

town hall, peeling and pocked from numerous bullet holes like a green walnut that is pricked full of holes before being stored for winter. Next to it stood a large gray building, which, strangely, was not as damaged by the violence of war. This had once been the police station. On it now hung a wooden sign. Red, badly painted letters spelled out: MILITIA.

"Militia," Koko read aloud. "Mama, what is 'Militia'?"

"The police," the mother replied, and by her voice he could tell that she had no intention of further explaining that unusual word. He thought for a while, looked again at the red, slanting letters, and ran after his mother, who was already climbing the stairs.

The room that they entered smelled of tobacco and boots. Two tall, lean men in uniform walked up and down, while a third, somewhat plump and puffy in the face, sat at a table examining a pile of papers. He continually wiped the sweat from his round, smooth forehead with a big, gaudy handkerchief. As the restless pacing of the other two quieted down, he lifted his head and noticed the woman with the boy.

"What is it?" he asked in a gruff voice. "What can I do for you?"

Mrs. Milich related briefly all that had happened at Green Hill, adding that the inhabitants of the village were afraid that the robberies would continue.

"There are only a few houses up there, and they are fairly separated from one another. Some of the men have not yet returned from the war, while those who are at home work all day long, so that they sleep soundly at night. We really don't know . . ."

"Yes, yes," the plump man interrupted, while gazing worriedly at his handkerchief, which was drenched with sweat. He was thinking that he did not have anything else with which to wipe his perspiring forehead and face. "Only, what can we do about it?"

"You could try to catch them. The thieves, I mean."

"And do you suspect anyone?"

"No, we have no idea who it might be. If we at least had a suspicion, it might be easier. . . ."

"Well, then we can't do a thing," said the plump man, and smiled broadly. "What do you think, Lovro?" He turned to one of his two comrades. "How would it be if we started chasing chicken thieves, huh?"

All of them laughed. Mrs. Milich looked abashed, and she was about to leave without saying a word when the man who had been addressed as Lovro stopped her with his serious and friendly tone.

"Don't get us wrong. The sergeant was only fooling a bit. These days we are really not yet able to help in such cases. After all, one can say that the war ended only yesterday, and every minute things are happening where we must pitch in and help. The town is still full of solitary enemy soldiers, and sometimes we find even a handful of them. Yesterday they killed three peaceful citizens near the park. You see, it is clear that we are needed more here. Don't be angry, but at this time we cannot help you. We do not have enough men. In two or three weeks maybe we can do something, but for now we really cannot."

Mrs. Milich thanked them, feeling sorry that she had resented the apparent unconcern of the good men, and went out, pushing her son before her.

"That means nothing doing," said Koko, looking his mother in the eyes. "That's about it, isn't it?"

"You see that they can't. People are still being killed. So it really isn't important if someone is stealing chickens."

"And what if they had killed me last night?" the boy thought to himself. "What would they say then? Would it be important then?" He imagined himself lying motionless and bloody in his white bed. He saw the whole horrible scene before his eyes so vividly that he involuntarily shuddered. He had to hurry now to see his friends as soon as possible and to tell them his troubles.

"What's the matter with you? Why are you trembling?" his mother asked in surprise, stroking his rumpled hair with her wide, callused palm and worn fingers.

"Nothing, nothing at all. Let's hurry. I would still like to take a swim in the lake before dinner."

4

Whispering in the Willows

The four boys had their fill of grapes. Only Cockroach was still nibbling as he lay on his stomach and tried to pick off a grape here and there from a bunch with his two middle fingers. The other three sat in the shade of a lonely pine at the edge of the vineyard. Blacky and Tom were playing a game to see who could spit the farthest. Bozo sat deep in thought, wiping his glasses with a grape leaf. He was secretly glad that they had lost the ball yesterday and could no longer play football. Because of his awkwardness, he never took part in the games.

Suddenly a whistle was heard from below. One long and, right after that, one short. It was Koko giving their signal.

All four jumped up. Koko came running. He stopped at the pillbox, shaded his eyes with his hand, and spied his friends. "Hi," he cried in a hoarse voice, and coughed. "Hi!"

"Hi!" Bozo shouted back and went ahead of the rest like a herald.

Koko waited for them on top of the pillbox. It looked as if he wanted to make a speech. That is exactly what he would have done had not Cockroach stopped him beforehand.

"Well?"

"Has Bozo told you?"

"Yes, we know everything. What happened at the police?"

"Did he tell you what happened last night? How they . . ."

"I know, I know," the owner of the blue bicycle repeated sharply. "We heard everything. All the same, you made up

that part about the green handkerchief, you dope. Everybody knows that robbers wear black handkerchiefs, that is, if
they don't have masks."

Koko's eyes bulged with surprise. Had he really mentioned
a green handkerchief? But since he was not quite sure what
he had blurted out to his shortsighted neighbor, he decided
that it was wiser to accept Cockroach's correction.

"Yes, it must have been black. It was hard to see in the
night. Besides, I had just waked up. Come on, let's go to the
willows," he suggested. "It's awfully hot here. I'd like to get
wet a bit."

He sprang from the pillbox and raced down the embank-
ment toward the lake, pretending not to notice the curiosity
of his friends.

"Come on, come on," Blacky spoke up angrily, nevertheless following him, as did the other two. "Don't act so smart!
Tell us what happened at the police?"

"Militia, now it's called the militia," Koko replied, and
stretched out on a flat spot in the midst of the thick, high
willow shoots.

"It's all the same," said Cockroach. "What did they tell
you?"

"They told us that they cannot do anything for now, that
they must still chase after enemy soldiers who are murder-
ing innocent people in town. And they said that they don't
have the time now, they don't have the men . . ."

"Hm," Blacky said seriously. "Of course, the war has just
ended. . . ."

"He said that we at least ought to know whom we suspect. . . ."

"Huh, wise guys! Even my little brother could catch them
then," Blacky shot back angrily again. "Maybe the thief is
one of those enemy soldiers who is hiding out in this forest."

They looked at one another confusedly and stared at the
dark oaks that stood like soldiers around the blue lake. Tom

even crawled forward a bit on his knees so that he could be closer to the other boys.

"Yes, that's possible," Koko uttered grimly, angry that he had not thought of it first. "I'm going into the water a while. We have to go home soon anyway."

"Wait," said Cockroach, getting up suddenly, and then he squatted and somewhat mysteriously shut his big green eyes. It was evident that he intended to say something especially important. That is why he waited, so that his words would make the deepest possible impression.

"What?" Koko inquired, scratching himself behind the ear while trying with one hand to take off his pants, which were too tight for him.

"I think," the green-eyed boy continued in a sonorous and solemn voice, "I think that we could do something about it!"

"We?" Tom came even closer to the rest, gazing apprehensively at the forest, as though he expected an enemy soldier with a helmet over his head and with a bloody bayonet at the end of his rifle to emerge from there.

"Of course, we," Bozo replied calmly, as though the question had been put to him, for he regarded himself as the author of the idea. "We can do a lot. We could find out who the robber is, and maybe we could even catch him."

"No," Cockroach said hotly, taking the role of organizer into his own hands. "It's plenty if we find him out."

"Nonsense!" Blacky spoke up and spat over a willow branch into the water. "Nonsense. Kid stuff."

Koko felt that the conversation was becoming interesting, and the suggestion excited him. How often they had wanted to undertake just such a well-planned, bold, and exciting venture. So he put on his pants again and said significantly:

"Besides, the policeman said that we could get a reward for just identifying the thief."

Blacky sat up. Nobody doubted that Koko was telling the truth, least of all he—at that moment. They began to talk in whispers, like real conspirators. The rustling of the willows merged with the murmuring of their muffled voices. Only occasionally someone would get overenthusiastic and let out a loud yell, but the reproachful glances of his fellow conspirators would quickly shut him up. Bozo and Cockroach came up with numerous possibilities. Koko put in enthusiastic comments and shouts, Blacky gave sober, practical advice, and Tom sat, gaping and speechless, and only glanced at the forbidding forest from time to time. They decided to get to work that very night. They could do nothing in the daytime because thieves appear only at night.

When at last they got up, the sun had already gone a good distance past the middle of the bright sky. They walked more carefully than in the morning, almost on their toes. All of their faces were unbelievably solemn. Older, one could say.

Then something occurred that made an unpleasant impression on the young conspirators. They no sooner got up and began to leave their green hide-out than Tom quietly gasped.

"Look!" he exclaimed, and pointed toward the lake.

Not far from them, only a few paces away, sat a hunched figure in a black threadbare coat. From behind they could see the wide part in the middle of his gray hair and his red scalp. The fishing pole that the man held was motionless, as though it was stuck into that aged, impassive body.

"Isaac!"

"Busybody!" Blacky exclaimed furiously. "I'd like to know how long he's been here. Maybe he's heard everything, even though he's pretending to be deaf."

It was old Isaac, who lived in the ramshackle shed at the edge of the forest, on the southern side of the lake. The children always avoided him and were just a little afraid of him.

"Hello, good day," Blacky called halfheartedly. "How's the fishing?"

The old man slowly drew the hook out of the water and shook his head on noticing that the bait was gone. Just as they were about to call to him again, he half turned his head around. They saw his nose, which was as crooked as the fish-hook that he held in his hand.

"Hello, children. Poor, poor. I have been sitting here already for two hours but not a nibble. I wonder if there are any fish at all in this puddle."

The boys were full of consternation. It was clear that he had heard them. Maybe he had not understood everything, but he could tell what was going on. Yet it was important that no one should know their secret—especially not such a suspicious character! Well, from now on they would have to be more careful. Much more careful.

"Good-by, sir," Blacky said again, and turned with the rest toward the forest.

Cockroach got on his bicycle and, winking, cried:

"Tomorrow at nine."

"Nine sharp," Bozo replied for everyone.

5

The Myth about Black Coffee

Cockroach sprawled in a deep armchair, trying to pay attention to what he was reading. He had some prewar newspapers, full of comic strips, which his sister's fiancé had brought him and which he had already looked through several times, but never had they seemed as stupid and as uninteresting as now. No matter how much he tried to grasp the predicament the hero was in, on the edge of the roof, exposed to the bullets of some gangsters who were popping out of the chimney, he could not believe that anything of the sort ever really could have happened. He felt, perhaps for the first time, that real life can be more interesting than fiction. Occasionally, he glanced at the big open windows. The sun had already set, and the red afterglow was slowly burning itself out on the horizon. Night was falling.

The whole family was gathered together. Old Rudolf Leib, a painter who had been wounded in the leg during World War I and who always walked with a cane, sat in the armchair opposite his son, reading the newspaper. His wife, Margaret, was knitting at the table, while their daughter in the corner was absorbed in a thick novel.

"Aren't you going to eat anything?" the worried mother asked again, turning to her son, who was absent-mindedly watching the hero of the comic strip as he dangled from the top of a skyscraper.

"No, I don't want anything. My stomach hurts, I told you."

The old painter momentarily glanced over his spectacles and then buried himself again in the political news. Cockroach's sister sighed. Night was falling faster.

"Rudy!" The woman turned suddenly to her husband. "I think we ought to get another dog as soon as possible to protect both the cow and the horse. We also have pigs and firewood."

"Ye-e-e-s . . ." Leib drawled without lifting his head from the newspaper, and then all of a sudden he sat up straight. "Listen, surely you don't believe in those stories about the thieves, do you?"

"Everybody is talking about it. They robbed Lucy . . ."

"Which Lucy?"

"Lucy Bobich. Oh, go on, as if you didn't know! Then last night they plucked the Miliches clean."

Cockroach raised his head. The conversation had become interesting.

"Harrump!" The head of the house snorted. "A chicken thief wanders in, and right away the womenfolk set up a howl: robbers, robbers. I sleep lightly, and thank goodness for that gun that we found in the orchard. If anyone so much as sticks his nose into our yard, he'd better watch out. Besides, we have a high wall around the yard."

"Don't take it so lightly. We might come to grief over it. We are the ones in this region with a horse."

"Oh, now, now! We'll talk about it some more later. Just let me read my newspaper."

Cockroach was thinking that this time, strangely enough, his mother's opinion was the more reasonable one. Anyway, his father would wise up when he saw that more was at stake than the chickens, that perhaps somebody might get hurt. Besides, the poor man didn't know that he, Cockroach, had sold the gun long ago to Tom's brother Ivo. "If things should become very dangerous, I'll have to warn the old man," he said to himself, and stood up.

"Are you going to sleep, Vincent?" his mother asked, unraveling the yarn. "Don't forget to brush your teeth."

"No, I won't forget. And don't call me Vincent. You know that everyone calls me Cockroach."

His sister giggled, and his father coughed meaningfully.

"I'll eat a little fruit in the kitchen," Cockroach added, as though he had not noticed his sister. "They'll be thanking Cockroach when they find out . . ." he thought to himself.

"You'll find the pears and the plums in the pantry. Good night, son."

"Good night."

". . . night," old Leib mumbled, and settled himself more comfortably in the armchair. The sister did not say anything but sighed deeply once more, for the young count in the novel had just been skewered by the sword of a traitorous knight.

Cockroach quickly left the room and went toward the kitchen. He was not even thinking about the fruit. He wanted to get his hands on something else. In the pantry, which was located next to the kitchen, it was completely dark; the light bulb had burned out and they could not get a new one. He began to grope around. As his fingers touched a piece of cheese, he could feel his mouth watering. He was almost sorry that he had not eaten anything, but he remembered that in such moments one should not think about trifles. Besides, he had not been able to eat because he was so excited, and there was no sense in feeling sorry about it now. He continued to grope in the dark until he finally felt the smooth touch of a pot beneath his hand.

He knew that black coffee kept one awake and that no one drank it before sleeping. It was very important for him to stay awake the entire night. This had been the boys' agreement: to keep watch the whole night long, so that they would not miss out on anything that happened at home or in the neighborhood. Cockroach always fell asleep very promptly and early, so he decided to drink as much coffee as possible; it was powdered, which people said was stronger. Cockroach peered into the pot—it was full almost to the top. He lifted it to his lips and spluttered. It was bitter, without sugar. "So much the better, so much the better," he thought, and began to gulp down the vile liquid, grimacing and choking as if he were drowning.

As he climbed the stairs to the second floor, where his room was located, he felt his head spinning, and his stomach really began to ache. He clenched his teeth tightly and held on to the railing. There was a curious bulge under his shirt. It was the biggest kitchen knife they had.

He decided not to turn on the light in his room so as not to attract the attention of the robbers. If they came, they would notice only the lighted rooms: the dining room on the first floor and his parents' bedroom on the second floor. When the lights were turned out, the thieves would wait a bit longer and then approach the house, carefully watching the windows in which there had been a light previously. It would never cross their minds that on the second floor two green eyes would be watching them alertly through the curtains. Cockroach held the big knife behind his back. Too bad for anyone who wasn't careful and who made a false move that night!

Cockroach sat in a chair that stood against the wall between two large windows. One was open, the other shut, and both were covered with transparent curtains. He did not dare sit on the bed, since he was not quite sure of the magic power of the coffee. He looked at the pillow and thought how nice it would be to lay his head in its white softness. His head was becoming heavier and heavier, while in his stomach he felt a rumbling and a dull pain. He was beginning to feel sick. He gritted his teeth and decided not to think about anything except his duty. How shameful it would be if something happened and he were not awake!

How could he ever face his friends the next day? He opened his eyes wide and began to stare at the ray of moonlight that slipped through the curtains to lie in the center of the room.

He could hear his father and mother climbing the stairs. They were talking about something. Probably they had forbidden their daughter to read much longer. She slept in the dining room, on the couch. Cockroach stood up and, without moving the curtains, looked into the garden. The tops of the plum trees no longer reflected any light from the room on the ground floor. That meant that his sister had obeyed and had turned out the light, or else she had read the novel and now wanted to lie in the dark and think about her Milan, who had to stay in the barracks that day and who probably would not come for a visit before Sunday.

In the neighboring room—which was his parents' bedroom—a muffled conversation could still be heard. His father spoke in a calm, monotonous voice, while his mother spoke rather vehemently. They were most likely discussing the robbers. A few more words could be heard, and then everything was quiet. Through the crack under the door Cockroach could see that they had turned out the lights.

The youngster continued to look through the curtains a while, trembling with an inner chill when a big tomcat jumped from a tree onto the roof of the chicken house, and then he turned his gaze to the room. From a big picture that his father had painted and that showed some fish on a long plate, fish eyes stared into the room, and it almost seemed that they were blinking. On the other wall an antique clock with a long shining pendulum stuttered:

"A-ha, a-ha, a-ha . . ."

Cockroach wanted to stop the clock, but he did not know how without waking his parents. It seemed to him that he was hearing it for the first time. Conscious of its unexpected importance, the clock began to laugh quietly:

"Aha-ha-ha-haa, aa-ha-ha-haa . . ."

Cockroach's eyelids began to droop over his green eyes, and the ray of moonlight on the floor began to dance before his eyes. He stopped his ears to keep from listening to the bewitching laughter of the old clock. His stomach was beset with cramps, and he felt like putting his finger into his mouth to vomit, but he remembered that his parents might hear. In vain he tried to sit up straight on the chair. His head drooped lower and lower. It seemed to him as if he had already sat up the whole night and that the dawn would soon come. Staggering, as though he might fall any moment, he tottered to his bed and placed the knife on the night stand. Then, dressed as he was, he fell on the bed and went to sleep.

And so, on that particular night, Cockroach went to sleep thirty minutes later than usual.

6

Dream and Reality

The house of the Bran family was situated on the eastern side of Green Hill, that is, on the side opposite the lake and the little houses in which Koko and Bozo lived. Their next-door neighbors were the Leibs, and one reached them by the wide Green Hill Road, which led into town. But they could not see the house even of their closest neighbors, since they were surrounded by thick rows of pine trees. Theirs was also a two-story house, but the whole ground floor was given over to a large barbershop, the property of Mirko Bran, Tom's father.

When the family gathered at supper, it was already fairly late. They had waited for Mr. Bran to return from town, for his wife did not want to begin supper without him. Tom's brother Ivo was angry at this and with his two fingers had picked at the white part of a fresh loaf of bread, which was the only food already on the table. Around nine o'clock the black-haired barber, with a big thick mustache, finally came. Smiling contentedly, he patted his older son on the shoulder and winked at the mother. He paid no particular attention to Tom, but the younger boy was used to this, and it no longer hurt him. It had all begun, Tom believed, the day he declared that he did not wish to work in his father's barbershop but that he wanted to finish school and become a doctor. From that time on, his father began almost to hate him. He beat Tom for every little thing and then became indifferent, so that he took almost no notice of him. His father's contempt struck at Tom's heart only when he exhibited it before Tom's friends. Anyway, today's business must have certainly been good for Mirko Bran. He kept on smiling and said:

"Well, the time is past when we felt afraid and went hungry. We have waited a long time for this."

He even put his hand on his hip, stretched his mouth in a sour grin, and remarked, looking straight in the eyes of his younger son:

"If that kid was a doctor by now, maybe he could do something about this awful rheumatism of mine."

"Wait a little longer," Mrs. Bran said gently, bringing to the table a pot that was steaming like a locomotive. "Be patient. I have no doubt that our little Tommy will become a good doctor someday."

"I wouldn't let him treat me even if I were dying," Ivo said contemptuously, and solemnly stroked the sparse little mustache that had only recently made its appearance on his thin upper lip.

The supper was especially good: frankfurters with rice, something they had not had even a whiff of for four long years. At first Tom wondered what those thin sausages were, and then he remembered their name and sighed with satisfaction. Unfortunately for him, however, an exciting and dangerous assignment was awaiting him that night, and so he could not eat as much as he might have. Whenever he remembered the conversation about the enemy soldier, his throat tightened up and he had trouble swallowing the sausage.

"What do you say about the stories, Mirko?" Tom's mother suddenly asked.

"What stories?" Bran asked, talking with his mouth full.

"Those about the robbers, about the thefts. They are poisoning dogs . . ."

"Ah, those . . ." The barber mumbled unintelligibly.

"Well, it's possible. Anyway, they can't steal anything of ours except for a few chickens. I think,"—here he stuffed his mouth again—"that it is one of those runaway enemy soldiers who is hiding in the forest or somewhere nearby and who pilfers by night."

Tom choked and began to cough so hard that he had to leave the table. Never again, never again would he go by himself through that terrible forest, even in the middle of the day. When he returned to the table, he pushed away his plate heaped with rice and announced that he was not hungry at all. After a short while he asked in a quiet, husky voice:

"And what will happen if they poison our Hector, too?"

"Yes!" His mother's voice chimed in. "Tommy is right. They have already poisoned several dogs: the Miliches and . . . I think they have poisoned Leibs' Viking as well."

"Well, they won't poison ours. Just let them try," Ivo said calmly, as if there were something he could do about it. "I'd just like to see someone poison our Hector."

"Well, well!" Old Bran became serious. "As far as that is concerned, we really cannot be sure. That darned Hector would eat a poisoned rat just to sink his teeth into some meat."

"You see," his wife declared, "something ought to be done."

"Well, there's nothing we can do. We should keep watch during the night. I sleep downstairs next to the barbershop anyway. Ivo can move down with me, and we shall certainly hear if anyone comes. You—and the little one upstairs—don't need to worry about a thing."

The "little one" frowned angrily and stared at the heap of rice. He was proud that no one knew that the "little one" would stand watch alone and that he would save them from danger if anything happened.

"You know, they might be armed, too," Mrs. Bran reminded them fearfully. "You'd better be careful."

"Just let them come! We'll get after them with the razors. How about it, Ivo? What d'you say?"

"And with the scissors!" Ivo laughed and again stroked the wisps of his future mustache. "Just let them come."

Tom was truly proud of his secret, but he also wanted the family to find out as soon as possible about his great courage. True, he did not know yet what he was capable of doing, but he was convinced that he would do something unbelievably bold and wise. Anyway, he hoped it would happen soon, for he found it difficult not to give himself away. Furiously, he watched his brother, who was lazily gulping down his mess of cold rice and who was even helping himself to the frankfurters that lay on Tom's own plate.

Finally supper was over, and the barber announced that it was time to go to sleep, for they had to get up early in the morning. Business was picking up because people were finally able to give thought to their hair and their beards.

Mrs. Bran decided that she would wash the supper dishes the next day because she was very tired. Mirko Bran had begun, early in the war, to sleep downstairs in the little room next to the barbershop, saying he was afraid that someone might break in and steal his valuable tools. The bed was wide, so that there was also enough room for Ivo, who was apparently pleased that his father had so much confidence in him.

Tom and his mother went to the big bedroom, where there was no electric light, since the lightbulb had burned out. They lit a kerosene lamp, which hung over the bed.

"Mama, may I sleep in Ivo's bed?" Tom asked gaily when they entered the room. Until now he had slept in his father's big bed, which was in the middle of the room, right next to his mother's. Ivo's bed was by the window, not far from the door to the balcony.

"Oh, don't bother me now. I'm awfully tired."

"Mama, I would *so* like to sleep in Ivo's bed," Tom repeated, as though he had not heard his mother's reply. He was sure, as usual, that she would not refuse his wish.

And indeed, the mother said nothing more about it. To show his gratitude, Tom undressed much more quickly than usual and, covering himself to his chin, he whispered cheerfully:

"Good night, Mother dear."

". . . night, Tommy. Go to sleep now," the tired woman replied drowsily, and also lay down, but not before blowing out the light, which flickered and then disappeared.

Everything was completely still. When he became accustomed to the dark, Tom could see the blanket on his mother's bed rising and falling slowly and steadily. He could also hear her measured breathing. Just the same, to be absolutely sure, he called ever so softly:

"Mama!"

She did not move. There was no doubt that she was fast asleep. The poor thing, she certainly must have worked hard that day. Still, she was fortunate to have a son who watched over her and protected her.

Tom sat up in bed, propped his elbows against his knees, placed his head in his hands, and stared into the starry night. What were the rest of his friends doing? Were they being true to their plan? Were all of them standing watch? Was something already happening somewhere? No, surely nothing had happened yet. Nothing of this kind ever happens before midnight. To be exact, in stories these things always happen on the very stroke of midnight. If only there were a church nearby or if they could hear the striking of the clock in the next village!

Tom soon noticed that his eyelids were blinking faster. His head tried to slip out of his hands, but he firmly put it back in place and rubbed his eyes. He must not fail! Out-

side there was no noise at all; but this only made him all
the more sleepy. Looking in the direction of the window, he
saw countless stars, which shimmered like the shining surface of the lake in which he had swum so many times. Then,
suddenly, the stars disappeared and the blue lake really
came before his eyes. He was running toward it because he
was very warm and wished to jump into the cool water as
quickly as possible. All of a sudden he stopped at the very
edge of the lake, for he heard someone's heavy footsteps.
Quickly he turned around and spied a giant in a green
uniform: he had thick bushy eyebrows and a terrible threatening glance, which flashed above a black handkerchief. In
his hands there gleamed a long rifle with a bayonet. Tom
shrieked and ran into the water, while behind him he heard
the quick pounding of stamping feet. He ran through the
water as quickly as his legs could carry him, but he always
seemed to remain in the same place, in the shallow water.
The steps came nearer and nearer. Then, unexpectedly, he
could hear Hector barking, and Tom looked around again.
He saw his beloved dog running to his rescue in leaps and
bounds. The fur rose up along its back. But the awful-
looking criminal lunged at the brave police dog with his
bayonet. Horrified, Tom turned his head. He heard Hector
yelp in pain.

When he woke up, he could still hear the painful yelping,
but it was growing softer and shorter. Was that really Hector? His eyes bulging wide and his mouth agape, he lay in
the dark. How would it be if he called out? But what if it
were nothing? Everyone would laugh at him, and his father
would give him a licking to boot. Besides, he might thereby
give away their secret. However, the terrible dream did not
allow him to think. The next minute he was curled up again
and deep in peaceful and untroubled slumber.

Nevertheless, Tom had not been mistaken. That was the
last time that he was ever to hear his beloved Hector.

7

Black Phantoms at Work

"All right," Mary replied, and got up from bed. "Only you have to promise me that you will get a new big Gypsy as soon as possible."

"I will, of course," Koko declared firmly and reassuringly, getting up from his bed and touching the cold floor with his bare feet, "just as soon as I can."

"Honest to goodness?"

"Honest."

And so Mary agreed to change beds with her brother. As a matter of fact, she had always had a secret wish to sleep beside the open window, so that her brother's suggestion made her happy. Afraid that he might change his mind, she did not wish to show her enthusiasm immediately. Why did Koko do it? Perhaps he was afraid that what he had been telling his friends might really come true: the man with the black handkerchief and the cold knife in his hands! He did not wish to admit to himself that he was afraid.

"That was smart," Koko reflected. "They know from last night where I usually sleep. If they come tonight, they won't know what's what. They certainly wouldn't stab a little girl, for she is not dangerous. Besides, I can watch them better from here than from so close."

" . . . night, Koko." Mary yawned, breathing deeply in the fresh night air.

"Good night, Mary."

Koko lay with his eyes shut tight, and he marveled that he

was not sleepy. This made him especially glad, for he knew
that he would not lag behind his friends. What he did not
know was that at that moment all were already asleep. Bozo
had fallen asleep, despite a bitter battle with himself, as soon
as he touched his pillow; Cockroach had dozed off tortured
with cramps from the bitter coffee; Tom was fleeing in his
sleep before the enemy soldier with the huge rifle; and
Blacky had fallen asleep without even trying to stay awake,
for he did not believe that the robbers would come to his
place and, besides, he considered the whole plan rather
childish. Naturally Koko could not know that he was the
only one who was still awake.

He did not feel at all afraid (or at least he wanted to
believe this), and yet he tossed about in bed, possessed by a
certain uneasiness. He was almost sorry that he had changed
beds with his sister, since her corner was completely dark.
Finally he covered his head, hoping that sleep would rescue
him. But, alas, he remained awake as if it were daytime. He
pushed the blanket from his head and almost shrieked with
fright. A cloud had covered the moon, so that for a second
the little room had grown completely dark, exactly as if
somebody had stopped there or passed by the window. Drops
of sweat appeared on Koko's forehead. "Oh," he thought,
"how Cockroach would laugh to see what a coward I am!
Maybe even Bozo, maybe even he wouldn't be this frightened. He would have known right away that it was a cloud."

The boy finally opened his eyes and decided that there
was no sense in trying to go to sleep. Mary was breathing
heavily through her nose and sleeping with her arms beneath her head. Koko tossed about angrily. First he placed
both arms under the pillow, then only one; later he curled
up his legs, then turned toward the wall. "How long is it till
morning?" he wondered. "It must certainly be five o'clock
by now." Of course, it was not yet midnight.

Suddenly he sat up. There was no doubt about it.

Whether from fear or from tossing about, he must go outside. Their toilet was a ramshackle wooden outhouse on the
other side of the yard, not far from Gypsy's little house.
"Not far from the place where the robbers were last night,"
Koko thought. Then it occurred to him that it was a good
thing the robbers had come last night. Certainly they would
not come again tonight. Anyway, even Father had said at
supper that there was no more reason for them to be afraid
of a robbery, for they had nothing more for anyone to steal.
Surely the robbers would not come again. Koko was almost
glad that he had to go out into the yard. He could not sleep
anyway, and it must be nice outside.

Carefully he threw the blanket back, stretched, and stood
up. He decided not to go out through the door, for he
would wake up his parents, but through the window, since
theirs was a one-story house. He stood on the edge of Mary's
bed, regretting once more that he had not stayed in his own
bed. He stepped across his sleeping sister and crept to the
window.

The night was completely clear. Only here and there a
wisp of cloud floated in the sky. It was fresh, almost cold
from the rain in the afternoon. However, Koko had been
mistaken in one thing: it was not at all nice. In fact, it was
horrible. Every rustle of a leaf, every shadow caught his
attention, and though he was barefoot, nevertheless he
walked on his toes. "Here, on this very spot," he could not
help thinking. "It was here that the armed criminal came
yesterday."

Despite all this, everything went well. The only trouble
was he had to come back the same way. Trying to close the
creaky door behind him without making any noise, Koko
decided to run to the house. Then, suddenly, a strange,
vibrating sound filled the air. In the nearby forest an owl
was hooting. This trifle probably would have been of no
consequence had Koko immediately recognized the call of

this night bird. But at first he could not figure out what it
was, so he stood still in order to be able to hear better. He
recalled how often he had read in Wild West stories that at
night the Indians signaled to one another with various
animal calls. Thus he wondered whether this might not be
some prearranged signal. But it was no signal, and the next
moment he realized that it was really the hooting of an owl.
Meanwhile, standing and listening, he raised his head and
looked about him.

For a moment he stood as though rooted to the ground
and felt his knees and legs giving way beneath him. What
he saw amazed him so much that he thought he must be
dreaming. However, there was no doubt that it was really
happening. The owl sounded his vibrating call again.

The house of the Tonchiches, a good-natured, lonely pair
of old people who had neither children nor relatives in this
region, was situated somewhat to the south of the house
that belonged to Koko's parents. One had to go down a little
path along a gentle slope and cross the dusty Lake Road.
Then one was right in front of the rotting, leaning fence
of their run-down house. As Koko lifted his head, he saw
a pale light moving among the weeds in front of their house
and hovering for a moment above the path. Then it slithered around the house. First he saw the light, and then he
spied a rather tall, somewhat hunched figure that was evidently holding a flashlight in its hand. Then suddenly beside this figure there appeared another phantom, which was
carrying something white. This one was thinner and
smaller. Then both darted away, and the light went out.

Koko stood for a moment with his mouth agape and his
limbs frozen. Later he secretly marveled that he had been
so decisive and bold. Quickly he ran through the yard,
jumped over the fence, and set out for the Tonchich house
along a bypath. He intended to come from the western side,
knowing that there was some tall corn and many bushes

there. As he ran, he wondered why he could hear no barking, but he remembered that their dog Bundy had also been
poisoned last night. Having reached the corn, he hesitated
for a moment, but then he thought how triumphantly he
would tell his friends the next morning about the unbelievable events of this night. That thought conquered his
fear, and he went among the tall cornstalks, whose rough
and bewhiskered ears of corn grazed and tickled him.

Soon he had made his way through the corn and dashed
into the bushes, from which he could watch the nearby
house. In the twinkling of an eye he saw what had happened. The door of the attic, to which steep wooden stairs
led from the yard, was thrown wide open, and from it
dangled a broken lock that still swung slowly to and fro.

Of course, there was no longer a trace of the thieves. Still Koko was filled with pride. Here he was on the scene of the crime just a few minutes after the thieves had left. He started for home, erect and with easy strides; nevertheless, when he came to the road, he crouched and scooted across and, making a wide arc, returned to his own yard. Again the tireless owl sounded forth.

Once there, before going through the window, Koko turned around again and looked toward the robbed house. He felt chilled. Not far from the bushes in which he had hidden just a little while ago stood the taller of the two phantoms. Koko felt his legs about to buckle under him, and his mouth went dry. As quick as a cat, he leaped through the window, shut it after him, jumped across his sister's bed, lay down, and covered his head. For a long, long time that night he trembled so hard that the springs of the bed creaked. Since it was summertime, he was certainly not shivering from the cold.

8

Suspicions in the Morning

When Bozo woke up, he immediately realized that he had not kept watch for a single solitary minute. Everything in front of his eyes was still misty and rosy, so that he had to feel around uncertainly on the chair by the bed. Finally he found his glasses, wiped them with the edge of the bedsheet, and placed them on his nose. The hazy outlines of the room were transformed into walls, windows, and objects. It was early morning.

Bozo's mother, a seamstress who worked in town during the day, was already up, cleaning and mending. The lad was ashamed of his laziness and unconcern, and so he quickly leaped out of bed, even though he regretted leaving its pleasant warmth.

". . . morning," he muttered drowsily, approaching his mother, whose diligent, incredibly swift fingers were mending an enormous hole in the heel of his sock.

"Good morning, son," the woman replied, bending over and touching the top of his head with her lips. "Did you have a good sleep?"

"Yes, Mother," Bozo replied on his way to the yard to wash himself in a big bucket of fresh cold water. He took off his glasses before picking up the soap, and again all around him became one hazy blur. His mother was saying something from inside the house, but he could not quite make it out because his ears were full of water and soapsuds.

Only after he managed to clean them did he cry out loudly:
"What did you say, Mama?"

"Last night the Tonchiches, too, were robbed. Their
whole wash taken from the attic . . ."

Bozo, who was just then wiping the soap from his neck
and holding his head in the bucket, banged his crown
against the wooden rim. "Fine, and I slept through it all!
Fine," he thought.

"The poor woman washed all their clothes and linens
yesterday, but she could not put them out to dry because
of the rain in the afternoon. And now she doesn't have a
single thing."

"Who told you?" Bozo asked, drying himself furiously,
even though he had not rinsed properly.

"The milkman, who always goes there before he comes
here. He says that the old woman is sitting and crying her
eyes out, while the old man cannot get out of bed, but is
shaking and groaning. I feel so sorry for them . . ."

"We should have prevented it!" Bozo suddenly declared
as soon as he had put on his glasses again, and he clenched
his fist and stamped his foot on the ground.

"Who? We?" The mother smiled gently when her frail
son appeared at the door. "We?"

"Oh . . . you don't understand. Anyway, it makes no
difference." He shook his head helplessly and wandered
about the room as though looking for something. Naturally,
he was not looking for anything. He was only upset and
angry. He did not doubt at all that Koko knew everything.
Nevertheless, a new idea was taking shape in his brain.
Maybe it was not completely new; maybe it had begun to
occupy his mind yesterday.

"We ought to look out for our few poor little chickens.
Tonight I will let them into the kitchen. And . . ." His
mother was silent for a while; then she continued in an
unusually gentle voice. "I think that it would also be a good

idea to keep an eye out during the day. . . . You could stay at home a bit more often."

"Yes, sure. But today I can't, at least not this morning. We already agreed . . ."

"Of course, of course, you go right ahead. First drink your coffee. It's on the stove."

Bozo hastily drank the coffee, which was too hot and burned his tongue. He kissed his mother, who gave him the key to the house, and finally he went out with big strides. He walked with his head held high. "Just a little longer," he thought, "just a little longer, Mother, and I will save you from all these worries."

He was about to whistle for his neighbor Koko when he saw him coming straight toward their yard, carrying in his hand an empty pail. Since their pump had been stolen, the Miliches drew water from the Tuciches' little well.

"Bozo!" Koko shouted rather strangely.

"Do you know what has happened?" Bozo said instead of a greeting.

"What?"

"Last night they robbed the Tonchiches, too."

Koko laughed and set the windlass on the well to turning while he lightly held it back with his hand.

"Do I know?" he said through his laughter. "Why, I saw everything."

Bozo could not utter a word. He might have known it! Koko had seen everything! Shame, shame. Nevertheless, he would not admit that he had fallen asleep right away. He did not like to lie. But this time he would have to.

"What did you see?" he asked as indifferently as he could, but making a sour face, which evidently made his friend even happier.

"Oh, it's not so easy to say, not at all." Then suddenly Koko became serious. "I was nearly . . ." He made a mo-

tion with his hand as though his throat were being slit.
"They nearly got me."

"Who? How many were there?"

"Last night there were two of them. One was tall, a bit
hunchbacked, the other small . . ."

"A bit hunchbacked, you say?" Bozo took notice. "Of
course."

"What of course?"

"Nothing. Just like that. Did you recognize them?"

"No, don't be funny. If I had recognized them, it would
all be over by now. They wore masks," he concluded in a
higher voice. "You know, when I came close and when I
wanted to . . ."

"You know what," Bozo suddenly interrupted him. "You
tell me all about it later. Go to the lake and tell the gang
what happened, and we shall see what can be done. We
certainly have to do something."

Koko was a bit offended that his neighbor did not want
to listen to his adventure of last night, but still he agreed,
happy that he would astound all the rest.

"Good," he said, drawing the bucket from the well and
pouring the water into his pail. "And you?"

"I'll come a bit later," Bozo said significantly, adjusting
his glasses and not looking at the speaker but rather at the
clear water in the pail. "There's something I have to do
first. I'll hurry."

They separated immediately. Bending over the load in
his right hand, Koko was thinking. Then he lifted his eyes
and spied Bozo as he briskly walked along the road and then
turned toward the forest. "Funny," he thought. "Funny."
He shrugged his shoulders and set out for his house.

Meanwhile, Bozo knew exactly where he was going. On
coming to the big bend in Lake Road, which turns here to
meet the main highway leading to town, he stepped from

the powdery dust into the freshly mown grass and started toward the forest edge.

"If what I suspect is true, then everything will be very simple, very simple," he repeated to himself, trying to tread on as many blades of grass as possible with each step of his bare feet.

He went along the very edge of the forest until the end came in sight, and then he turned left along a narrow well-trodden path. Before him there was a clearing, which did not seem to be a part of the old oak forest at all. Behind the young supple trees, mostly acacias and witch elms, a thin column of black smoke rose up like a threatening forefinger.

A little shack came into view. A hunchbacked old man was splitting wood over a big log. After every blow he took a deep breath, trying to raise himself erect. This was old Isaac's home. But Bozo did not seem at all interested in the old man. His restless eyes sought something else. He came a bit closer to the shack, around which there was neither a fence nor a yard.

"Good morning, sir," he called in an unnecessarily loud voice.

The old man was startled, and he looked nervously about until his dim eyes spied the lad who had greeted him. Then his furrowed eyebrows separated slowly and gently.

"Hello, sonny! What brings you here?"

"Have you seen Koko, Koko Milich, anywhere around?" Bozo inquired while his eyes wandered over the leaning walls of the shack, over the woodpile next to which a goat was standing and bleating.

"No, I have not seen him. Maybe he went by while I was still asleep."

"Probably. I have to find him. His mother is looking for him."

All of a sudden the black nose of a dog peeked around the corner of the shack. It was old, almost blind Hobo, old

Isaac's only companion. Bozo jumped on noticing him. The dog slowly approached, sniffed him over, and then happily wagged his tail. Isaac stopped chopping wood, took a file out of his pocket, picked up a big knife from the log, and began to sharpen it. The grinding sound caught the boy's attention. As he looked at the old man, it seemed to him as though his face reflected something evil, something as cold and as hard as the knife that gleamed in his hand. Bozo quickly lowered his eyes, glanced at the dog, and spoke rapidly.

"Never mind, maybe he has already gone home. He probably gathered enough tinderwood and went back. If you should see him, tell him, please, to go home right away."

"I will, sonny!"

"Good-by, sir!"

"Good-by, sonny!"

Bozo turned and began to run. When he reached the forest, he stopped, smacked his fist into the palm of his other hand, and declared half aloud, "That's it, that's it! We should have known right away."

Isaac, too, immediately stopped his sharpening, turned his head, and placed a gnarled hand on the head of Hobo, who was sitting beside him. It seemed as though the old man also suspected something and was thinking.

9

True Lies

"As soon as I saw them, I knew it must be the robbers,"
Koko was saying as he knelt and looked around, as though
afraid that someone might be listening besides the three
boys who were lying in a circle.

"And then?" Cockroach asked, green in the face and
holding his stomach, for it still hurt. "Huh?"

"Then I made a big, big circle around the road, got down
to the cornfield, and began to crawl, all hunched up." Here
the storyteller imitated the crawling by falling on his hands
so suddenly that Tom jerked back and could hardly catch
his breath. He even stopped thinking about poor Hector,
whom they had found this morning stretched out in front of
the garden gate. Blacky, who was studiously watching a
rather long cloud that looked like a submarine, looked
contemptuously at the group before him and spat as far as
he could. This disturbed a hornet that was hovering over a
yellow flower, and it began to buzz and to dart through the
air.

"When I looked again through the corn, I didn't see
anything, for there was no one in front of the house. Then I
decided to steal through the bushes, which are a bit closer
to the house. I went through the bushes and looked out. At
that moment"—here the lad stopped and looked at his listen-
ers with a significant glance—"a knife glistened in front of
me."

"Eee-e-eek!" Tom shrieked and then reddened, ashamed of his cowardice.

"What?" Cockroach said unbelievingly.

"He's lying!" Blacky snapped, trying to blow away the hornet, which, it seemed, insisted on landing on his nose.

"I'm lying, am I? O.K., so I'm lying. But didn't they steal the Tonchiches' laundry from their attic, huh?"

"They did. But you heard that this morning. And last night you were sleeping. Just like me and just like all the rest," Blacky replied, waving his hand and sitting up, inasmuch as the hornet had become more insistent. "I knew that our plan was no good."

"I didn't sleep," said Cockroach, and began to yawn, as though to prove it.

"Nor I!" Tom declared cheerily, and clapped his hands.

"No, you didn't. That's why they poisoned your dog under your very nose, you poor dunce." Blacky flared up and hit the hornet with his hand, so that it finally flew away and sat on the petals of another flower.

"But . . . I could hear nothing . . . I . . ."

"Tell us mo-o-ore," Cockroach drawled, forcing himself to yawn. "You know Blacky; he never believes anything."

"When I saw the knife"—the offended storyteller was glad to continue—"I drew back right away. But I wasn't careful enough. They must have heard me. I didn't see them any more, but I heard one saying softly, 'Did you hear something?' The other one answered, 'No, what?' 'There's something there in the bushes.' 'It must be a cat. Aim the light over there.' I crawled backwards as quickly and as quietly as I could. The bushes were thick, and the light could not reach me. Otherwise . . ."

"Say, did they wear black handkerchiefs?" Cockroach interrupted.

"Handkerchiefs?" Koko repeated. "They wore masks, real honest-to-goodness black masks, with narrow slits for their eyes. Just like in that movie we saw that time, remember?"

"I thought so," Cockroach said with satisfaction.

"You didn't recognize them, of course?" Blacky inquired, whirling his legs in the air as though he were riding a bicycle.

"No, I didn't recognize them; one was tall, the other short."

"When two men are together, usually one is taller and the other shorter. You really are . . ."

Blacky wanted to say something else, but suddenly he howled and jumped, so that the other three sprang up and stared at him in amazement.

"The devil! He bit me, darned bug!" Blacky shouted at the top of his voice, hopping about on one foot while clutching with both hands at the sole of his other foot. He limped off to the lake and stuck his bitten foot into the water, muttering all the while.

The boys looked at one another, not sure just what to do. Knowing the nature of their friend, they thought it best to pay no attention to him. Strangely enough, it was Tom who first gathered his wits.

"What will we do now?"

"With him?" Koko inquired in a low voice, pointing with his thumb across his shoulder in the direction of Blacky, who was sitting motionless on the bank.

"Not with him, with the robbers." Tom spoke in a frightened tone, pronouncing the last word with special care.

"Well, we have to do something. Something more daring, something more serious. First of all, we must arm ourselves; then we must set up an ambush," Cockroach began, and not knowing what should come next, he shut up and stroked his stomach, from which strange sounds were again emanating.

"But," Koko said all of a sudden, and scratched himself

behind the left ear, "it seems to me that that cockeyed Bozo knows something, only he won't say yet. This morning he acted very queer, as though he had expected everything to happen just like it did last night."

"What could he know?" Cockroach's green eyes stared wide.

"Here he is. Bozo is coming!" Tom shouted, and clapped his hands for joy.

"Now we'll hear," Koko concluded, and waved his hand to the newcomer, who certainly was not yet able to see them at that distance.

10

Five Blades of Grass

Bozo was coming with long strides and did not run only because he was afraid to lessen the impression he would undoubtedly make with his proposal. At first he spotted a bright blur dancing on the green grass, and then he recognized that it was a hand that was waving to him. He then slowed down a bit and began to gaze at the clear lake and the enormous oaks as if he didn't care. He first came upon Blacky, who was still holding his foot in the water, and his face reflected indescribable fury and outrage.

"Hi!" Bozo greeted him gaily, but inasmuch as he received no reply, and seeing the black look on the sitting boy's face, he shut up and went on toward the group of boys who were eagerly waiting for him.

"Hi, fellow!" Cockroach hailed him good-naturedly, moving the bicycle, which lay in the grass, to make room for the newcomer to sit down as close to them as possible. "What did you dig up?"

"I?" Bozo inquired diffidently, looking to see where he would sit down. Trusting his hands more than his eyes, he felt for a spot. "Koko told you what happened, didn't he?"

"Yes," Cockroach replied quickly. "That's not what I mean. He says that you know something more."

"What do you mean, I know something more?" Bozo turned to Koko, feeling his position becoming more and more important and interesting. "Hm?"

"Nothing . . ." Koko was confused. "It seemed to me

. . . this morning . . . somehow you didn't seem surprised enough."

"Maybe I do know something," Bozo stated mysteriously, and the eyes behind his thick glasses narrowed. "That is, maybe I suspect someone."

Nearby there was a ripple and a gurgle. It was Blacky, who had lifted his foot out of the water and was carefully examining his sole, twisting himself completely so that he could bring his curious eyes as close to the stung spot as possible. The smile on his long, lean face eloquently declared that the wound was not dangerous. Limping along on his good foot, he approached the other four boys, who sympathetically watched his funny ambling.

"A wasp?" Bozo asked, as if he had forgotten all about the question that had just been put to him.

"Hornet," Blacky replied quietly, and sat down.

"Go on, talk, and stop acting so smart," Cockroach prodded.

"Tell us," Tom followed up fearfully.

Once again Bozo looked gravely at all present, opened his mouth to say something, then closed it again, and finally began with this significant question.

"Have you suspected anyone at all yet? I mean, someone we know, someone around here?"

All looked at one another in wonder and slowly shook their heads. Only Blacky lowered his eyes and again examined his swollen sole.

"You said that one of the two was tall and hunchbacked, didn't you?" Bozo turned to Koko, who was glad that he could be of help because of his experience last night.

"Yes, one was tall and slightly hunchbacked."

"And rather old?"

"I'd say he was on the old side."

"And he limped a little?"

"It seems to me that he did limp."

"And his voice was rough and hoarse?"

"Yes, it did seem hoarse." Koko was happy that his friend knew he had heard the man's voice.

"Like an old man's?"

The questioner fell silent and again carefully scrutinized all his friends who were sitting around him. In their eyes there was really something akin to amazement, and this the lad with the hooked nose and shortsighted, clouded eyes had never experienced before. He was fairly bursting with pride when he asked again:

"You still can't guess who it might be?"

Nobody could guess as yet. Even the unbelieving, aloof boy whose foot was smarting turned his head and listened carefully to the unusual conversation.

"Is your Hector still alive?" Bozo turned suddenly to Tom, who almost fell backward with surprise.

"No . . . he isn't . . ." he barely gasped. "They poisoned him last night."

"Aha!" the young investigator declared with a voice still full of meaning. "They have poisoned Hector as well! As far as I know, they have poisoned Gypsy, Hector, Cockroach's Viking; then they poisoned Lucy's dog, Bundy, and Radichs' Lola. Blacky, you don't have a dog, do you?"

"No, we don't."

"That means that they have poisoned all the dogs, all—except one."

"Which one?" they all asked at the same time.

"Old Hobo," Bozo said softly.

"Good old Hobo!" Tom clapped his hands with joy that at least Hobo was still alive.

"He's blind as it is!" said Cockroach contemptuously. "Anyway, what does that have to do with the robbers?"

"Isn't it strange," Bozo asked again, rubbing his knees, "that only one single dog is still alive? True, he is blind, but he might be fiercer than some other dog. He is blind, but he can smell all right!"

"How do you know that he wasn't killed last night?" suddenly asked Blacky, who was becoming more and more interested in this information.

"I was just there." ·

"And you think that that man is the thief, that is, that he is stealing along with someone else?" Blacky asked unexpectedly, and pointed with a finger across the lake. On the other shore, limping and bent with the burden of his years, old Isaac was walking, carrying two fishing poles and leading Hobo on a leash.

No one could utter a word. Even Bozo was dumbfounded at his friend's keenness. Nevertheless, he was the first to speak up.

"It isn't strange at all that someone doesn't want to poison his own dog, is it?"

As everyone looked at him silently, he continued with his explanation, as though he were arguing with someone.

"Isn't he hunchbacked? Doesn't he limp? Isn't his voice rough? Besides, I ask you, how does that man make a living?"

"He saws wood," Tom mentioned cautiously.

"Saws wood, saws wood! What if he does saw wood? What can he earn doing that, I ask you? Can anyone make a living around here by sawing wood two or three times a month?"

All were silent and lowered their eyes. They were almost a bit disappointed that the thief had been discovered so quickly and simply—and that it was not they who had discovered him but that numskull with the glasses!

"The last time he was at our place," Koko spoke up as though he were reading from a book, "when he sawed wood, he said that we had a fine pump. And that wasn't so long ago."

"Yesterday he sawed wood at the Tonchiches'." Cockroach

smacked himself on the forehead. "He knew that they had washed clothes and could not dry them because the rain had begun. He probably found out that they were going to dry the wash in the attic overnight."

"Listen, fellows," Blacky declared suddenly, standing over them like a column. "I think that that guy"—he pointed to Bozo—"is darned right. Anyway, he is smarter than all of you emptyheads put together. It seems to me that over there is the man we're looking for."

Again they all stared at the hunched figure in the black coat who sat quietly on the bank of the lake, calmly watching the cork bob on the blue water.

"Only," Blacky continued, "we have to prove it. Besides, we have to catch the other one, if he really exists and if this guy didn't make him up. Maybe he's the main one and the old man is just his assistant, his partner."

"Yes, that's what I think," said Bozo, and stood up in order to show that he too was making the decisions here and that he was next in importance to the tallest and oldest among them.

"Ambush!" Cockroach blurted out, remembering his earlier idea.

"What ambush!" Blacky snapped, and spat as far as the water, even though he was just half turned toward the lake. "It would be enough to trail him, to watch him at night, and maybe we will discover the other one, if he exists. Only one person can do that. Of course, it would be best if one of us did it. It would be easier, and he would not be noticed so easily."

"That's it!" Cockroach exclaimed joyfully, and smiled broadly.

"That's it," Tom repeated like an echo.

"Who shall go? When?" Bozo asked.

"Whoever goes ought to go tonight. As for who is going

to go, we ought to draw straws. That is the only fair thing to do."

It was daytime, and it didn't seem to any of them that it would be especially terrible to trail that old man who was fishing so peacefully on the opposite shore. But, at night, that would be something else. Ever since last night, Koko and Tom and Cockroach all realized this. Besides, this assignment would certainly prove to be more dangerous. They all agreed to draw lots.

Blacky plucked five blades of grass. The one who chose the shortest would carry out the dangerous mission that

night. They all sat in a circle, with Blacky in the middle. From his fist there stuck out five green ends, which were completely even now. The first to draw was Bozo—in alphabetical order.

"That's it!" said Blacky on observing that Bozo had picked a blade that was no longer than half an inch or so. He opened his fist and showed the remaining blades: all were much longer.

11

The Old Man and the Dog

The sewing machine droned on monotonously and lazily. Judging by the sound of it, one would think that it did not have the strength to make another single turn. It strained and struggled, creaked and groaned. Kate Tucich, Bozo's mother, whose fingers were already scarred from frequent pricks of the needle and whose back was bent from working steadily over the sewing machine, was particularly tired that day. She had spent the whole day working, and now, though it was evening, she had more to do for some of her friends and for herself. Every once in a while she would shake herself in an effort to keep from falling asleep. Once she really did fall asleep, and the sharp needle of the machine nearly went through the thumb of her left hand.

Her eleven-year-old son was pacing up and down the room rather excitedly. From time to time he would go to the door that led into the yard, or he would stand in front of the window or move into the kitchen. Most often, however, he would stand in front of the window, examine it, even climb up on it, and jump into the yard, returning through the door. "That's good," he thought. "I can even jump in my shoes without anyone's hearing. If I don't wear shoes, then surely no one will be able to hear."

As he jumped through the window a second time, his mother began to watch him in wonder. Finally she smiled and asked:

"What's the matter with you? Are you trying to find out

whether the thieves could jump in? They surely would not dare do that. Besides, they know we have nothing."

"What makes you think that they know? How would they?"

"Ah, these are no thieves from afar. It must be somebody who knows well how we live—somebody who saw that the Tonchiches had put their wash in the attic. The only thing of ours that they could take is the sewing machine. But that is a little too heavy."

Bozo fell to thinking, turned toward the open door, gazed into the night, and smiled. He was happy that his mother thought as he and his friends did. Naturally, she did not suspect who it might be. Nor did the other inhabitants of Green Hill suspect anything. Those who had not yet been robbed would again go to bed that night with fear in their hearts. Just that night. Tomorrow morning everything would be all right.

"There's some buttermilk in the kitchen. And there are several pancakes left over from dinner. Take them if you want. I ate in the shop."

Bozo did not care for supper, even though pancakes with jam were a particular favorite of his and appeared rarely on their modest table. Nevertheless, to keep his mother from wondering even more at his strange behavior, to keep from rousing her suspicion, he hastened into the kitchen, discovered the pancakes, and began to stuff them into his mouth. His fingers were sticky from the purple-plum jam, and he licked them with delight. My, but the pancakes were good! He took the glass of buttermilk and, unable to stand it any longer, returned to the room and stopped before the window.

It was completely dark by now, and the ragged edge of the forest was barely distinguishable from the murky sky, for the slender moon was covered by a cloud. The buttermilk was not yet quite sour and did not taste at all good after the sweet pancakes.

"Mama," Bozo suddenly said, without turning around. "Where did that old Jew come from? How did he make a living before?"

"The woodcutter?" his mother asked, not lifting her eyes from the apron she was stitching, which wriggled in her hands as though alive as it passed beneath the swift needle. She was not surprised at the question.

"Yes, the woodcutter."

"Who knows? People tell all sorts of things about him. He has been here for quite a long time. They say that he was once a tailor or a barber, something of the sort. I once asked him about it, but he wouldn't say. Some claim that he is not a Jew at all, for if he were one, he could not have stayed here during the war. You know that they persecuted the Jews and sent them to concentration camps."

"Well, what is he then?"

"The same as you and I and all the rest of our neighbors. They say that he got the name Isaac because of his hooked nose. That is why people began to believe that he is a Jew. Anyway"—here the seamstress lifted her head and looked at her son, who stood motionless by the window—"what makes you think of him now? Hm?"

"Oh, just like that. Today, when we were at the lake, we were watching him fishing there. A queer old man. I just don't see how he makes a living."

"Well, people help him. Besides, he eats the fish from the lake. He has a goat. It seems to me that he does not need much. For a while"—Kate smiled—"people used to say that he had some money stashed away, that he had a rich brother somewhere. But I never believed it."

The boy made no reply. The moon had emerged from the cloud. It was cool, clear, and still.

The seamstress heaved a deep sigh, leaned her elbows on

the sewing machine, and put her head in her hands. Then she got up quickly and said:

"Son, let's go to sleep. It's late! I can hardly keep awake."

"Let's go, Mama."

Mrs. Tucich was glad that her son agreed so willingly to go to bed. Generally he protested loudly, claiming that he was no longer a child of five and that he did not want to go to sleep with the chickens. She was too tired to realize that Bozo might have his own particular reason.

Soon both were in bed, but Bozo did not take off his glasses. Instead, he lay on his stomach and leaned on his elbows, so that sleep would not catch him unawares. He could see and hear that his mother was already asleep. He smiled as he noticed that she had pulled the sewing machine right up to the bed, within reach. She was afraid of the thieves after all. "One more night, just one more night," Bozo thought.

It was not long before he decided that it was time for him to go. If his mother should wake up by any chance, he knew what he would tell her. He would say that he was going to chase the chickens into the kitchen, as she had intended to do but forgotten. He cast one more glance at his mother's bed. She was sleeping soundly.

Bozo slipped from the bed, carefully touched the cold floor with his bare feet, put on his short pants and shirt. In his pocket his fingers felt a box of matches. Then he remembered that a white shirt would be more noticeable in the dark than his tanned body, so he took it off and placed it on the bed. Casting one more glance behind him, he tiptoed to the window, climbed up, and jumped into the yard, into the night. Everything was all set. He could now embark on his great venture.

He left by the yard gate and found himself on the road. He wanted to turn off immediately, but somehow he felt easier and safer on the road. The forbidding somber forms of the giant oaks, which he saw to the right of him, filled him with something like terror. When he came to the curve, the same spot at which he had turned off that morning, he realized that there was no going back now. He left the road and began to tramp through the high, uncut grass, which tickled his thighs and behind his knees.

Then suddenly he remembered something. A light breeze was bending the grass, and the whole forest seemed to move with the swaying of the tall treetops. From time to time there was a strong gust of wind, while the clouds, which gathered more and more, were scurrying across the gloomy sky. The boy wet a finger and lifted it high in the air. He felt the touch of a cool breeze to the right: the wind was blowing from the west. Perhaps it was a little thing, but resourceful Bozo could not afford to overlook even little things. Blind Hobo had an excellent sense of smell, and it would be good to approach him on the side from which the wind was not blowing. Otherwise, the whole venture might fail.

Bozo went back to the road again, followed it straight east until he came almost to the Tonchich house. There was the cornfield through which Koko had crawled the night before. Bozo turned his back on the house of the robbed old people and set out through the same cornfield, only in the opposite direction. As soon as he reached another clearing, he crouched and, quick as a rabbit, ran the distance to a little clump of trees that surrounded Isaac's dwelling from almost all sides. Before he entered the green thicket, he looked once more at the sky. Thick clouds had already swallowed half the Milky Way.

Once in the thicket, he walked very slowly at first, hanging on to each tree trunk within reach of his hand. He was struck by the fear that perhaps he was going too slowly, that he might come too late. What if the old thief had already begun to prowl? He had to go faster. He began to jump over the gnarled roots and almost tried to run. Only he was careful not to step on any dry twigs so that the sound of their snapping would not give him away. Suddenly a clearing was visible through the trees, and he recognized the poor shack. He took two or three steps more and stopped. He took off his glasses, wiped them on his pants, and stuck them on again. Strangely enough, he saw better at night than during the day.

Through a dirty little window there shone the pale light of a kerosene lamp or a candle. In a ramshackle shed of branches lay the goat. Around the corner of the house could be seen the hind end of Hobo's thick body. The big fancy tail wagged rapidly, as though the dog was expecting someone or saw someone—someone whom Bozo could not see from the other side because the shack was in the way.

"So," Bozo thought, "so! I was right. Only patience." From the nearby forest came the sound of an owl. Of course, Bozo knew that it was not an owl. He was convinced that this was a secret prearranged signal.

And indeed, just then the door of the shack creaked open. Hobo sprang up, and now the boy could see him dancing in one spot, standing on his hind legs like a colt and wagging his tail with all his might. Then he heard old Isaac's voice.

"Now, now, we're going, we're going. Only be still!"

Soon his bent figure also appeared in the pale moonlight. With a wave of his hand he quieted the prancing Hobo and tied a leash around his neck. The man and the dog set out. From the forest the owl could be heard again. The old man quickened his step and said softly to his companion:

"Come on, hurry up, there might be rain."

The bent old man really began to hurry, but the blind dog started pulling as though he wished to lead him somewhere. Bozo went around the little house, letting them gain some distance, and then followed them, going along the path.

"I thought so, I thought so," he repeated to himself. "Only, where are they going?"

Indeed, the man and the dog set out directly for the oak forest. They entered a clearing, and the boy had to wait until they came to the shadows of the trees on the other side. As soon as they did, he ran around the clearing in a big circle and entered the forest some fifty yards farther on. Then he ran until he spied them directly in front of him, making their way along the forest path. Luckily the leaves had not yet begun to fall, so that Bozo could move about noiselessly, even though he did not take the path. When he saw that they would come out right at the lake, he realized immediately that they were not going to go robbing that night. "Maybe they have a hiding place somewhere here where they stash away the stolen goods. Anyway, it's important that I see who the other one is! The one pretending to be an owl!"

Just at that very moment he heard directly overhead the flapping of wings, and the ill-boding night bird landed on the lowest branch of a tall oak. He stared right at the boy with his penetrating yellow eyes, so boldly and threateningly that the lad lowered his eyes. The bird shook the feathers on its head and sounded forth its mournful cry. "It was a real owl all the time," the disappointed lad concluded, and quickly went after the old man, who had already moved a good distance away.

When Bozo caught sight of the lake, the old man was already at the bank. Once more the boy took off his glasses, again wiped them on his pants, and began to watch intently to see what would happen now. Isaac stood for a while gazing at the sky. Then he quickly began to take off his clothes: first his coat, then his trousers. His bare bony body had the appearance of a skeleton in the meager light of the crescent moon. Hobo sat calmly beside him and stared at the water. Bozo could not believe his eyes. The old man went into the

water and swam toward the middle of the lake! Then he turned back toward shore. The dog greeted him by bringing him his towel. Judging by everything, Bozo concluded that the nocturnal bath was over. Amazed as he was, the boy might have watched this unusual scene for a long time more had not a gusty wind roused him. Now suddenly it began to blow from the east, so that the hair on Bozo's head stood on end. Hobo grew stiff, pricked up his ears, and began to growl softly. It was apparent that the wind had filled his nostrils with the smell of an unknown body.

Bozo quickly turned around and began to run. Though it already seemed a bit funny to him that he had suspected this harmless old man, still he decided to carry out his assignment to the end. Running breathlessly, he quickly reached Isaac's lonely shack. He had to look inside. Maybe behind those rotting boards there was hidden everything that had been stolen in the last few days.

But he no sooner found himself before the shack than his last doubts vanished into thin air. He realized immediately that something was wrong. Something was missing here. And then suddenly he realized: the goat! It was the goat that was missing. The thieves had taken advantage of the situation while the poor old man had gone to bathe in the lake.

Bozo stood rooted to the ground for a moment longer, and then ran home by the shortest route. The first big drops of rain began to plop.

12

Again New Plans

They had agreed the day before to meet at Bozo's early the next morning. Tom set out from home, whistled, and called Cockroach. The green-eyed lad came running, without having washed or eaten breakfast. The rain had stopped just half an hour before, and a muddy brook was flowing along the wide concrete highway. The sky was almost clear.

"Hello," Tom cried.

"M-m-m," Cockroach replied through his teeth.

The two boys walked along the road in silence, dodging the puddles of water. They strode as fast as they could, for both were burning with curiosity to find out what had happened the night before, or rather what their friend with the glasses had found out and seen. They were both thinking the same thoughts and thus did not feel the need at all to converse with one another.

Before turning off the highway onto the mud road, they had to pass in front of the Radich house. This is where Emmie lived. She had completed the fifth grade, and everyone thought her a real beauty. The entire school, and even the entire region, adored her. This time the two boys could not take notice of such trifles. Cockroach, who secretly sent her letters, and Tom, who blushed furiously whenever he looked at her, were not able to think of her now. There were more important things on their minds.

However, something attracted their attention, and both looked up. On a little balcony overlooking the crossroads sat Emmie's Aunt Anna crying. The boys exchanged embarrassed glances. It was Cockroach who finally gained enough courage to ask cautiously:

"Good day, neighbor. . . . What has happened?"

If she had not been Emmie's aunt, perhaps he would not have asked; he might not have dared. Perhaps something had happened to Emmie! The weeping woman took her hands from her face and looked down on the highway. Then she covered her face with her hands again and replied in a sobbing voice:

"Oh, children . . . our pigs . . . oh, oh, when my sister finds out . . ."

The three big fat pigs were the pride of the Radiches. Every year, while Emmie's father was still alive, they raised several pigs. They would keep some for themselves and sell the rest at the market before winter. Now that the family was without a breadwinner, that was almost their only source of income. Emmie's mother was not earning anything. She used to sell tickets at the movies, but the movie theaters were still closed. The time had not yet come to think of such things.

"So they stole your pigs!" Tom gasped, remembering the fat porker with the black ears of whom Emmie had been especially fond.

"All . . . they took all of them. . . . Oh, I was so afraid that this would happen . . ."

The two friends looked at one another again angrily. This was really going too far. If they only knew what Bozo had found out! They bade farewell to the weeping woman, took the muddy Lake Road, and set out for Bozo's house. They walked faster and faster, without looking where they were stepping. Both were splashed up to their knees. They no sooner came to the bend in the road than they saw that the other three boys were already in Bozo's yard, so they started running.

Blacky was arguing and waving his arms about a great deal; Koko was leaning on the fence from the other side, while Bozo was spreading bed sheets on the ground. Last night, in order not to wake up his mother, he had lain down in bed, wet as he was, and in the morning he did not get up until she left. Of course, everything was wet, and he was sneezing terribly, lifting himself on his toes each time.

"We're right back where we started from," Blacky snapped, breaking a sunflower with his left hand.

No one even noticed the two boys who came running breathlessly. However, they soon took care of that.

"The Radiches were robbed!" Cockroach gasped as he struggled for breath.

"All three pigs . . ." Tom added.

Their friends turned toward them immediately.

"When?" Koko asked unnecessarily, and then was ashamed of his question. Not knowing what else to say, he blurted out without any reason, "There!"

"There? Dumbbell!" Blacky was quite furious. "Oh, it's hard to have to work with such dopes. I have a sensible suggestion: let's invite Ivo to join us."

Ivo, who had just turned eighteen, who was growing a mustache, and who smoked away from home, was fifteen-year-old Blacky's hero. He yearned for his friendship and was ashamed of being seen at play with these kids whenever Ivo passed by. All, except Cockroach, were two or three years younger than he.

"No," Tom suddenly protested, exhibiting a firmness that he had never shown before. "We won't mix my brother into this. He would only make fun of us. No, we can do without him."

That Ivo would make fun of them was something Blacky did not doubt. Thus he was unable to say anything more. He decided to keep quiet and bent his head. He did not care much for all this. Besides, he no longer believed that they would get a big reward. "In any case," he thought, "a fifth of the reward would come to a very small sum at most."

All were silent and gazed at the ground. It seemed to them that it was all over now. Suddenly Tom started, clapped his hands, and asked:

"And Isaac? What about Isaac? What's up, Bozo?"

Cockroach also perked up and regarded Bozo. Not moving his head, Bozo peered over his glasses, sneezed, and replied in a hollow voice:

"Last night Isaac took a bath in the lake. It seems to me that he takes a bath every night. Besides"—here he paused a bit—"besides, meanwhile someone stole his goat. They probably knew about that habit of his."

Again silence reigned. Now there was really nothing that anyone could suggest. Cockroach thought of the clever detectives in the funny papers and tried to imagine what they would do in such a case. "That's dumb," he said to himself. "That is imaginary, but this is real life. What can we do?" Then suddenly there came before his eyes several pictures at which he had been looking the night before, just before he went to sleep. His heart beat faster.

"Hey, fellows!" he shouted as though calling someone. "I have an idea."

All except Blacky turned their serious faces toward him. He said at once:

"Why, we don't have to catch them at all!"

Their heads immediately fell again. Blacky blew contemptuously through his nose and turned away, as though he had caught sight of something interesting on the road.

"I didn't know you were such a dunce. Who ever said we had to catch them?"

"Yes, yes," Cockroach hurried on. "I didn't mean that. That isn't what I wanted to say. I meant . . . I wanted to say that it would be enough if we had their pictures to give to the police . . ."

"The militia." Koko corrected him as the wooden sign with the red letters hovered before his eyes.

No one said anything to this, for none of the boys knew how it was possible to get pictures of thieves. Blacky, the oldest boy, thought that it was superfluous to comment on such a stupidity.

However, Cockroach was insistent.

"We don't have to take a close-up. It can also be from a distance. . . . Anyway, it would help. The police . . . the militia might be able to do something then . . ."

"Listen." Blacky turned again angrily. "Listen, you long-eared pumpkin head, what will we take their pictures with?"

"With a camera," Cockroach replied calmly, as though it was self-evident.

"And *where* are you going to get a camera, if I may ask?"

Cockroach thought a while and replied sadly, "Yes, that's the only thing . . . we don't have one . . ."

"Dunce . . ." Blacky hissed, and spat in a sunflower's face.

Again silence reigned. One could feel the steam from the wet bed sheets. There was not a breath of air anywhere. In the Miliches' yard, Mary was trying to catch a bright-colored butterfly with a handkerchief.

After a long time Blacky suddenly laughed.

"Well I know where we can get a camera. Mario has one."

They shouted with joy, and Tom clapped his hands.

Mario was a queer fellow, a poet who was well known many years ago, they say, but who later passed into oblivion. Perhaps a reason for this was that he was not a real poet. Sometimes one could hear the sounds of a piano pouring through his open windows. They said that he played beautifully. He lived in a fairly nice house, a little beyond the Radich house and Lucy Bobich's house. From here one could see the roof of his house through the branches.

"Only"—Koko scratched himself behind the ear—"Mario

is a tightwad. He won't give it to us. Besides, he'll ask what we want it for."

"Pooh, who says he'll lend it to us? We'll take it!"

"That's stealing! . . ." Bozo was horrified and sneezed, getting up on his toes. "We aren't going to start stealing ourselves, are we?"

"Not at all. We shall borrow it; only he won't know that we borrowed it, and later we shall return it." Blacky laughed, but to himself he thought: "We'll see about that! The camera is probably worth a lot of money. If the reward should be small . . ."

"But who knows how to take pictures?" Bozo asked cautiously.

"I do," Cockroach replied gaily. "We used to have a camera, but we sold it during the war."

"I have still another idea." Blacky spoke up again. "Cockroach, your house hasn't been robbed yet, has it? You have a very high wall with pieces of glass stuck on top."

"No, it hasn't been. They only poisoned Viking."

"If you leave the gate open and put some bait in the yard, they will surely come to your place, maybe even tonight. What do you say?"

"Hey, that's wonderful!" Cockroach shouted. "Who will get the camera?"

"Listen." The fifteen-year-old leader of the gang lowered his voice and looked about cautiously. "We have to plan everything well. Two of us will get the camera. At all costs, understand? And one will go to Emmie to find out exactly what happened. Maybe there is something we ought to know. Maybe they suspect someone. Who's going to get the camera?"

"I will!" Bozo spoke up first.

"No, you won't. You were on the job last night. . . . Let Cockroach and Koko go. And let Tom go to Emmie's. Agreed?"

"Couldn't I go for the camera?" Tom begged hesitatingly, blushing.

"No," Blacky retorted. "That job calls for more skill. Well, then, are we agreed? Bozo and I will wait for you here. Hurry up!"

"O.K.," said Cockroach, feeling that the most important task had been assigned to him. "Let's go."

"What am I going to ask?" Tom was still protesting.

"Whatever comes to you, dope. Ask them if they have any ideas, if they suspect anyone, when it happened, whether they heard anything. Get it? Ask them if they found any strange objects."

There were no more questions to ask. They had to hurry as quickly as possible, for the clouds had gathered once more and the rain might start again any minute. The three lads ran to the road.

"Hurry up!" Blacky shouted once more, and spat at a sunflower.

13

Carelessness

When Emmie's aunt, Anna Radich, returned from town, she was more desperate than ever. At the police station they had told her that they were still unable to do anything in this case, even though they were thinking about Green Hill. The very evening on which her pigs had disappeared, in the town precinct in which this police station was situated, some stores had been broken into and two men attacked. Obviously the help of the authorities was still more needed elsewhere. Nothing could be done yet for the troubled inhabitants of this village.

Emmie cried at first, but then she began to comfort her aunt and tried not to think of her favorite white pig with the black floppy ears. Her aunt, all sighs and sniffles, started to clean the room, and Emmie stood on the balcony, looking down the road. That is how she saw Tom and waved to him happily, trying to smile.

"Come over here a while," she greeted the bashful caller, "if you're not going anywhere in particular."

"I'm coming," he replied, blushing terribly and looking at the ground.

"I'll come down right away. Come through the garden."

Tom pushed open the entrance gate and went in cautiously. Then he remembered that the Radiches' dangerous dog was no more, and so he stepped forward courageously, going around the house.

Emmie met him, her eyelashes still wet with tears, which

she wiped away with her fist. Tom no sooner saw her than
he begun to blush again and stared somewhere past her into
space. The rain began in a slow drizzle again.

"Let's go into the hay shed," Emmie suggested.

Tom followed her. On the way, he tried to remember
what he was supposed to ask her. The assignment that Blacky
had entrusted to him was still not entirely clear in his mind.
What was the good of all this? He and Emmie no sooner sat
down on a bench in the shed than he spoke up stupidly.

"So, they stole your pigs, huh?"

"Yes," Emmie replied, "but let's not talk about that."

Now it was up to him to say something bright, or else
everything would be a flop. He again lowered his eyes and
said importantly, gravely:

"I came to talk about just that. It is important. For you,
and for me, and for the rest."

Her brown eyes widened at these mysterious words.

"But . . ." she stammered, more confused than the questioner, "why should we talk about that? What good is it?"

"Yeah, what . . ." Tom began, but stopped himself short,
realizing that that was exactly what he must not say. "It is
important. I . . . I . . . cannot tell you why."

"Well, all right." Offended, Emmie pouted a bit. "How
shall we begin then?"

"Did you suspect anything? Were you afraid this would
happen? Did you find anything? Any sort of object?" He remembered Blacky's advice.

"No-o-o, we didn't. But why such questions?"

"And do you suspect anyone?" Tom spoke seriously.

"No, whom would we suspect? What are you anyway, the
police?" Emmie laughed. "Or maybe you're going to catch
the thieves yourself!"

Tom looked at her askance, blushed, and said nothing in
reply, while she continued slyly:

"You're hiding something. If you tell me what is going on,

maybe I can tell you something. But be careful; tell the truth!"

The boy was silent. After all, what if he did tell her their secret? Nobody else need know. Sooner or later everything would come out into the open anyway. His one fear was that his friends would find out. Then they would give it to him! Blacky especially would be angry. However, Tom wanted to show Emmie what important things he was doing and that his older friends trusted him. That would certainly impress her, and probably no harm would come of it. Why not tell her then?

"Well?" she asked, cocking her head.

"Hm," Tom muttered without raising his eyes from the ground, where he was watching a beetle. "Will you give me your word of honor that you won't tell anyone?"

"I won't give you my word of honor, for my mama told me that I mustn't. She says that it isn't very nice. You'll get used to it, she says, and then you will give your word of honor for every little thing. But you can believe me when I say that I won't tell anyone."

"Honest?"

"Honest."

Tom started talking. He told everything, failing to mention only Koko's nocturnal adventure, afraid that Emmie might be too enthusiastic over his friend. Instead he told her how he spent the whole night in his yard, walking around with a big knife in his hand. He added that they knew the thieves were heavily armed and that they wore black masks.

"And they poisoned your Hector anyway!" Emmie exclaimed sadly.

"They poisoned Hector anyway," the storyteller repeated sadly, and blushed. "I heard a noise, went from the yard into the orchard. There was no one there. And when I came back, Hector was already done for."

"Poor Hector!" The brown eyes nearly welled over with tears.

"Poor Hector," Tom repeated, and continued with his story. He told how they had suspected Isaac, how they thought that he had eavesdropped while they were talking about their plans; then, smiling, he told of Bozo's experience of the night before and finally mentioned that they were now going to photograph the criminals.

"And where will you get the camera?" Emmie asked in disbelief.

"Mario has one."

"Pooh, he'll never give it to you."

"I know. We are going to take it. Koko and Cockroach have already gone to get it."

"That's stealing!" Emmie said in horror. "Then you're thieves too!"

"We're not either!" Tom pounded the bench with his fist. "We're going to return it. And we shall pay for the film! We have to have it. We'll be able to discover the thieves through the pictures. We can tell their height, their build, how many of them there are."

"Oh, naturally," Emmie remarked, and fell to thinking.

Meanwhile, Tom remembered her promise and went on sharply.

"You said that you would tell me something! I've told you everything. Now you tell me what you know. Maybe you can help us a lot."

Emmie kept still.

"Well?" the lad insisted. "What about it?"

"And what if I don't tell you anything?" she retorted, smiling naughtily. "What if I don't know anything?"

"Then you tricked me. That isn't fair."

"Then I tricked you. But you won't be angry, will you?" Her brown eyes shone, and Tom was again as red as a ripe tomato. He stretched his foot and with the point of his shoe nudged the beetle. The little insect disappeared into the grass.

"No, I won't be angry," he said softly. "Only, don't tell anyone. You won't, will you?"

"No, I won't. You can be sure of that."

"Well, then, let's go!" The unsuccessful investigator spoke sadly, getting up.

"Where to? Where are you off to?" Emmie asked. Then suddenly she struck her forehead, as though she had just remembered something. "Oh, yes. This was an assignment! Now you're supposed to report on everything that you found out, isn't that it?"

She laughed loudly while Tom stared intently at the ground, searching for the runaway beetle. Had he spied him, the poor little creature certainly would have perished under his heel. Tom thought about his coming meeting with Blacky. What would he tell him? Shame! Oh, shame!

Hastily he said good-by and hurried across the yard toward the road, paying no attention to the rain.

Emmie stared after him a while longer; then she smiled slyly. She knew something. Rather, she knew what she was going to do now. She ran quickly toward the house.

14

It's Hard with Poets

"Shall we?" Cockroach asked in a whisper, trying to conceal himself completely behind a thin plum tree.

"Let's go. I'm ready," Koko replied.

A dismal rain had fallen almost the entire morning and afternoon, as though signaling the end of summer and the coming of a dreary autumn. Mario had spent the whole day at home. From a distance the lads watched him come to the window frequently and press his large red nose against the misty glass. It appeared that the rain annoyed him too and that he wanted to get outside as soon as possible. That was just what the two lads were hoping for.

A little before seven o'clock, just as dusk began to fall, a strong wind arose, which drove away the clouds. In about ten minutes the sky was blue and clear, like the sea in a calm. Soon Mario appeared at one of his windows and gazed at the sky. He was dressed, and it appeared that he would go out any minute. Indeed, he came out immediately, treading carefully so as not to step in a puddle. Most important of all, he did not take the camera with him! It meant that the precious instrument was still in the house. The plan was a very simple one. They were only afraid that the poet might close all the windows. However, the most important one was left open: the one they could get to by climbing along the rain pipe. It was already fairly late. Night was fast approaching, and they had to hurry. Their parents might get worried and suspect something. The boys abandoned the plum tree and scurried across a clear patch to the fence of the poet's house. It lay on the highest point of Green Hill, and from it one had a view of the entire countryside. They could see that Mario was going south, toward the little woods that hid the house of Lucy Bobich and Emmie. Who could tell how long he would remain there?

"What's he going there for?" Koko whispered.

"Who knows?" Cockroach replied somewhat louder. "It's hard to understand people like poets. Maybe he is just going for a walk, to watch the sunset. Anyway, let's get to work! He might return soon."

"Let's do just as we planned!"

They had decided that Koko, who was somewhat smaller and lighter, would climb up the rain pipe into the house, while Cockroach would stand guard. Koko would try to find the camera as soon as possible. (Just like a real burglar, he had brought along a whole ring of keys, which he had found among his father's tools.) He would then throw the camera to Cockroach. After that he would look to see whether the poet had another roll of film. Cockroach had explained like an expert that the camera might be quite empty, or else that there might be room for only one or two pictures on the film inside. Who could tell how many shots they would have to take? Maybe only one would be good. Naturally, the extra roll of film would probably be somewhere near the camera, but if it was not there, Koko was to search as long as he could. In case of danger, the sentinel was to whistle twice.

The tall boy helped his friend to climb up to the rain pipe from his shoulders. Koko looked around once and scrambled up like a young squirrel. He reached the window, got his stomach over the sill, and disappeared into the house. Cockroach began pacing impatiently beneath the windows. He felt the muscles of his legs quiver and his eyelids blink faster. "It's a wonder," he thought, "that real robbers don't

go crazy. My nerves are all on edge. Now I understand what my father means when he says that his nerves are all on edge from worry."

Meanwhile, Koko was examining the room, which was in half-darkness. First he saw a huge black piano in the corner, then two leather armchairs and a table with two straight chairs.

Many pictures hung on the walls, and on the stove there stood a statue of a miner who was swinging a pickax. Then something slithered from the stove to the floor. It was a big gray tomcat. He started toward the window, stopped in the middle of the room, and with his orange eyes blinked curiously at the unusual visitor. But there was no time to take notice of old cats. Koko quickly went to the door of the neighboring room; it was not locked. In that room a whole wall was covered with shelves of books, bright with the re-

flection of the evening sky. Here, too, there were two armchairs. Against the left wall there stood two wardrobes
whose doors were open. On the opposite side was a long red
couch on which lay some crumpled newspapers and an open
book. In the middle of the room stood a little table covered
with papers; some even lay on the threadbare rug.

Koko approached the wardrobes, opened the doors wider,
and peeped in. All the shelves were in terrible disorder.
There was a smell of unwashed clothes. At the bottom there
was a veritable graveyard of bottles, from small, square ones
to long, slender ones. He could detect the smell of whisky or
wine. There was nothing here that the boy was looking for.
"I'm surprised that the camera isn't in plain sight," he
thought. "He's always carrying it around and snapping something or other." But the camera was nowhere to be seen.
Koko bent down and looked under the couch. A pair of worn
slippers lay there and nothing else. He searched through the
papers on the table. His glance fell on some verses, which
were carefully inscribed on a large sheet:

> Across the silver night the moon sails by,
> On the sly,
> Up on high;
> The stars will vanish by and by,
> Swallowed by the hungry sky."

The boy grinned, wagged his head pityingly, and went back
into the first room.

Meanwhile, Cockroach was growing more and more impatient. Mario might return at any moment. Besides, they
were probably worried at home by now over his absence. He
paced up and down more and more excitedly, gazing in the
direction of the woods to see if he could catch sight of the
poet.

Koko was terribly angry at the tomcat, who kept getting
tangled between his legs. The boy almost fell over him. He

looked on the piano; he looked under the piano, on the stove and behind the stove. No camera anywhere. Then he opened the other door and went out into the front hall. It was completely black here, and he had to wait a while for his eyes to get used to the dark. "It's unbelievable, but I'm not a bit afraid, and I don't feel funny at all. Even my knees are not shaking. That is probably"—he remembered—"because this is not *really* stealing. We are only *borrowing*. Just the same . . . he would kill us if he found out!"

"He'll kill us if he catches us," Cockroach too was thinking as he looked angrily at the window through which his friend had disappeared. He was sorry that he had not climbed up himself. He certainly would have found the camera by now. Unfortunately, he could not even call to Koko, for it would be heard. Darn it, there was nothing to do but wait. He stuck his fists into his pockets and began to walk up and down again.

Just then Koko felt the cold touch of a double-barreled rifle, which hung in the entrance hall, and he shivered. "He'd get after us with that . . ." he thought, and carefully took his hand away from the dangerous weapon. Then an excellent idea flashed into his head. He opened the door of the kitchen to get some light. In that instant he almost cried out with joy. On a hook, in a leather case, hung the camera. Quickly he took it, went back into the room and leaned through the window.

"S-s-s," he hissed in a muffled voice.

From below two green eyes looked at him, full of restlessness and impatience. Cockroach spread his hands, and the precious instrument landed neatly in his outstretched fingers. One flick of his forefinger and the box opened; one expert glance and Cockroach raised three fingers in the air. That meant Koko had to look for more rolls of film. This was even harder, for the boxes of film were smaller than the camera. Still Koko sighed with relief. The main

part of the job was finished. He returned to the entrance
hall, hoping to find some film there. But there was none. It
would probably be in one of the wardrobes.

Cockroach carefully examined the wonderful shining instrument, aimed it at something far off as though taking a
picture, and smiled with satisfaction. It would do. Only he
had to be very careful when taking the pictures. He must
not hurry too much. The job called for experience and skill,
and he was convinced that he had enough of both.

Meanwhile, Koko dug around in a mine of clothes and
empty bottles, but he could not find what he was looking
for. "The question is whether Mario even has an extra roll!
It's very difficult to come by these days, and it's very expensive," he said to himself. But he had to search everywhere to
be sure. If he could only find some! In the drawer of the
table there was nothing except cigarette butts, corks, and
pencils. On the bookshelves there was also nothing except
books and plenty of dust. Then he remembered that he had
not yet looked in the kitchen. He hurried there and again
stumbled over the gray cat. It was almost as if the cat was
getting tangled in his feet on purpose, to knock him down.

Cockroach began to grow restless again. It was quite dark
by now, and he had to open his eyes wide to be able to watch
the woods to the south. Besides, he had to guard the other
side as well, for the poet might return by a different path.
Suddenly, about a hundred paces from the house, he spied a
blue spot that was approaching rather rapidly: it was the
poet's blue shirt. Mario was returning! Cockroach whistled
softly and crouched low. He whistled again, then twice in a
row.

Koko was opening the drawers of the kitchen table when
he heard the whistle. He ran out quickly, slammed the door
after him, and in the twinkling of an eye was at the window.
Cockroach pointed south and ran north, firmly clutching the
camera in his arms. This was no betrayal; such had been

their agreement. There was no point in their running away together, for each had to go to his own house anyhow. Cockroach still had to prepare the "bait" for the thieves that Blacky had talked about that morning. Therefore, he ran quickly away and soon reached the beginning of his father's property, the largest on Green Hill.

Meanwhile, Koko did not panic. Cockroach had whistled and had run away immediately: that meant that Mario was quite near. Koko decided to wait until Mario passed beneath the window and disappeared around the corner. Then he would climb the stair and unlock the door. Besides, the darkness of the night was quite impenetrable by now, and a prowler would vanish from sight in a twinkling. Therefore, there was no need to get excited. The only thing that bothered Koko was the gray tomcat, whose orange eyes observed him carefully in the dark. He could hear footsteps in the yard.

Then something happened that no one could have foretold. True, the tomcat miaowed, but not even that could have been the reason for Mario's unusual behavior. He hesitated beneath the rain pipe, looked it over, and then glanced at the open window, at which, luckily, Koko was no longer standing. Whether it was his daily custom, whether he suspected something, or whether it was a mark of his poetic nature, he bent down, rolled up his trousers, and resolutely began to climb up the perpendicular rain pipe.

15

A Child's Tongue

Emmie stood long at the window watching the rivulets of rain run down the road beyond. She did not like the rain, and when the sky finally began to clear, she smiled happily. Besides, today the movie theaters in town had finally re-opened, and her mother had gotten back her old job as cashier. Emmie opened the door and went out on the balcony. She wiped the railing with her hand and leaned her elbows on it. Then she gazed off into the distance.

Ivo was coming down the highway whistling, so she heard him before she saw him. He was just the one she wanted to see. There were two most important reasons for this: first of all, she secretly liked the tall young man with the bright eyes who was already growing a real mustache, and she was always proud whenever he consented to speak to her; then, too, a week ago he had captured a fine crow with a big yellow beak, and she had already begged him to give it to her as a present. The young man had promised that he would give it in exchange for something else, but she had had nothing to offer him. However, this morning she had something, and she believed that he would agree to the exchange.

"Ivo!" she called.

"What?" Ivo replied listlessly, without stopping.

"I have something to give you for the crow. Want it?"

"What?"

"Come to the door. I'll bring it to you."

Ivo reluctantly agreed. He did not believe that Emmie

was able to offer anything really valuable. Nevertheless, he was in no particular hurry, so he came to the front door of the Radich house.

Emmie ran down quickly, carrying something behind her back. Ivo raised his eyebrows questioningly.

"Look!" Emmie said merrily, and exhibited a practically new brown cap with a visor. "What do you say to that?"

Ivo straightened up a bit and his eyes shone.

"The devil! Where did you get that cap?"

"I found it!" Emmie said mysteriously.

"Where?"

"My, but you're nosy." Emmie shook her head. "I'll tell you anyway. Only you mustn't tell anyone. Last night the robbers lost this cap, and I found it next to our pigsty. It was under the edge of the roof, so that it didn't get wet. And I cleaned it a bit besides."

"And you didn't show it to anyone?"

"Not to a soul. Your little brother was here. He even questioned me, whether I knew something . . . about . . ." Emmie covered her mouth, remembering that she must not talk about that.

"Tommy? What did he ask you?"

At first Emmie did not want to say anything. Ivo insisted. He became so interested that he promised to give her the crow for the cap. Moreover, he promised that he would catch her a live squirrel and that he would make a cage for the crow. And all the while his eyes shone brightly.

"And you won't tell anyone?" Emmie asked mistrustfully.

"I won't."

After all, Emmie thought, why not tell him? Nobody would find out, and she so wanted the crow! It would be wonderful to own a squirrel as well. And a cage! No, she could not forego that. Besides, she felt proud that she could do something for this young man with a mustache. Anyway, she had not given Tommy her word of honor that she would not talk about their secret plans or about their hunt for the thieves.

So she told all—about Isaac, and about the masks, and about the knives, and about Mario's camera and the pictures they were going to take, and about Cockroach's plan to leave open the gate to the yard in which they would place some bait for the thieves.

"Ha-ha-ha!" Ivo laughed at the top of his voice, stroking his thin mustache with his palm. "Ha-ha-ha. That's wonderful, that's rich! Ha-ha-ha."

Emmie was almost sorry she had told him. She had not expected Ivo to laugh like that and to make fun. She kept still and lowered her head. She looked at the cap in Ivo's hand and regretted that she had not given it to Tom. Maybe she could have helped them to discover the real thief.

"Those are some detectives for you!" said Ivo through his laughter. "Ha-ha-ha. That's really fine. Who would have said that I had such a brave brother! Knives . . . and masks . . . ha-ha-ha . . ."

"You won't make fun of him, will you? You won't tell him that I told you?" Emmie begged, on the brink of shedding hot tears of repentance.

"No, I won't!" The tall boy suddenly grew serious. "Maybe later, when he grows up a bit. Let him have his fun for now. As for the crow, I will bring him to you tomorrow morning. Thanks for the cap, Emmie. Good-by."

"Good-by!" Emmie said, gazing after him.

Strangely enough, Ivo did not go in the direction he had been following when Emmie called him from the balcony. He turned around and went back, toward his own home. On the way he stuck his newly acquired cap on his head. It was a bit too large, so that his ears were bent and spread out beneath it. One could tell by the way he walked that he was happy. He began to whistle again.

"Perhaps he won't give me away after all!" Emmie thought, standing the while at the front door, looking after him. "I'm really sorry that I told him."

Then she remembered the crow, the squirrel, and the cage. She looked into the sky. Even though dusk was falling rapidly, one could tell that it was going to be completely clear. It seemed to her that life could be very beautiful.

16

A Great Discovery

There was no time to think of anything. Something had to be done, and in a hurry. Koko saw that Mario had taken hold of the rain pipe, and he quickly drew back. The climber did not see him. But he still had to save himself. He ran into the hall and tried to open the door to the house. It was locked, and he could not undo the complicated fastening quickly enough. He felt suddenly weak. He must hide somewhere.

Outside could be heard a rumbling and creaking, a scraping of shoes against metal, and muffled grunting. Luckily the poet was not very good at climbing. Koko came back into the main room and looked it over hastily. One of the two big leather armchairs was standing in the corner, opposite the piano. He could hide behind it. He tiptoed across the room, softly moved the armchair even closer to the wall, and crouched down. The gray tomcat with the orange eyes carefully observed his every movement.

"Hey, how are you, little fellow?" the poet suddenly called as his head appeared in the window.

Koko was stunned. What could he do now? It was almost unbelievable that Mario had spotted him so quickly. However, what else could this question mean? He decided to wait a minute longer before saying anything.

Then from the window there came the sound of scraping, panting, and knocking on wood, as though someone were slipping. The poet entered the room head first and tumbled onto the floor, where he remained for several moments, breathing heavily.

"Little fellow, what are you doing here?" Mario said anew, rising from the floor. "Why are you crouching there? Come on, come now, over here. You didn't think I would come back so soon, did you?"

By now Koko's mouth was completely dry. What was he to do? He decided to peek no matter what happened. Luckily, what he saw gave him courage and calmed him down.

"That's right, little fellow, that's right," said the poet to the tomcat, rubbing against his legs. Koko sighed with relief. Clearly he had not been noticed after all. Mario stood up, stretched, and began to walk around the room. Then he went out into the entrance hall and into the kitchen, leaving both doors open behind him.

The lad behind the armchair peeked again, and crouching there on all fours, he almost bumped into the large head of the tomcat. For a time they stared into each other's eyes, and then both turned their heads. Koko wondered. If he stood up now and tried to reach the window, Mario might see him from the kitchen. In fact, he might come back into the room at that very moment. From the kitchen was heard the clattering of dishes, knives, and the creaking of doors and drawers.

Indeed, Koko had not been mistaken. It was necessary to wait for a better opportunity. The poet was coming back, carrying in his hands a plate full of cottage cheese and several green peppers and a little bowl of milk, which he placed on the floor, not far from the piano. He then sat in the armchair behind which Koko huddled and began to eat. For a while Koko could hear only Mario munching with a full mouth and the tomcat hungrily lapping the milk. The minutes passed by with painful slowness.

Finally the poet stood up again, pushing the armchair a

little so that it struck Koko lightly on the forehead. Now the triangle in which he found himself, bordered by two walls and the back of the armchair, was quite small. His situation was becoming more and more unpleasant and desperate. Mario went into the kitchen again. Now the gurgling of water could be heard. He did not tarry long this time, either, but quickly returned to the room and threw himself again into the same armchair. This time Koko was squeezed tightly against the wall. He heard a match strike and saw a cloud of tobacco smoke rise above the armchair. The sharp smoke tickled Koko's nostrils, and he felt an irresistible urge to sneeze. He held his nose tightly with both hands; the tears came into his eyes. In this uncomfortable position he had to wait further.

"Hey, little one, come here," Mario called to the cat, while settling himself comfortably in the armchair.

The tomcat quietly miaowed, but he did not obey. He approached his master, but he went around his master's legs and stuck his head into the narrow space between the wall and the armchair. He observed the unbidden guest with curiosity and miaowed a bit.

"What is it, little one? What do you see back there?" the poet asked, turning around in the armchair. "Surely not mice?"

Koko began to think feverishly what to do. In that moment of desperation and weakness, he almost decided to give himself up. "It's not mice. It's me!" That is what he would say. What would happen then? "And if he should take a look himself? Then it will be even worse," he thought. "And he'll do just that if this darned cat doesn't go away."

"Come, come, little one," Mario called in an impatient tone. "Don't make me get up for nothing. You'd better watch out if there is nothing in the corner."

Koko decided to take a desperate gamble. He leaned quite close to the gray head with the orange eyes, stuck out his

forefinger, and flicked the tomcat on his black nose with all his might. The animal yowled loudly, spat, and jumped backward. "Come what may," Koko thought, trying to breathe inaudibly.

"Will you look at him!" shouted the poet. "Have you gone mad? You're too old to play like that. I know very well that there are no mice in our house, but let's see."

"I'm done for! Now he'll go straight for the double-barreled rifle!" thought Koko.

Meanwhile, the poet got up quickly, so that the armchair shook, and began to walk around it. Just then his glance fell by chance on the window that looked south. While the boy, who was right next to him, was desperate at the thought of the long heavy gun, he gazed wide-eyed and openmouthed at something in the distance.

"Look, look at that light down there," he said in a completely changed voice, and sighed deeply. Then he went abruptly into the neighboring room, brought some paper and a pencil, and threw himself again into the armchair, and the only sound was that of a scratching pencil.

"He's writing poetry!" Koko thought bitterly, deciding that it was safe to breathe again, now that the tobacco smoke had blown away. "This can last till morning. Will I get it when I come home!"

Luckily, the inspiration did not last long. The papers landed on the floor; the pencil was hurled against the opposite corner of the room.

"It won't come, little one," said Mario. "But I don't care a bit. We still have something to do tonight, don't we? Did you see how well I can climb already? You gave me that idea when I saw you coming into the house that way the other day. Tell me, I'm pretty good at it by now, am I not? It will succeed, won't it?"

Koko pricked up his ears and opened his mouth. He even scratched himself behind the left ear. He began to get very much interested in this confidential conversation of the poet with his gray favorite. The tomcat, who had been rubbing his nose with his paw all the while, leaped into his master's lap. Koko could hear him purring beneath the touch of his master's hand.

"Do you think I could climb up *that* rain pipe as well? What do you say? Shall we try? Let's try this very evening! Shall we go together? The two of us: you and I. Like real thieves, like real burglars." Mario laughed uneasily. "All right? Hm?"

Koko could hardly believe his own ears. Was this really happening to him, Ratko Koko Milich? "Can it be that he, Mario, is the thief?" the boy thought in amazement. "That's why he climbed up the rain pipe! That was just practicing for a new robbery. Oh, if he would only mention his partner's name!"

Meanwhile, Mario did not mention his partner's name, but he did continue talking to the cat.

"If there is no rain, maybe we shall be able to do it even today. Shall we, hm? What a surprise that will be!"

"What a surprise it will be for you when we catch you in the act, that is, when *I* catch you in the act," said Koko to himself. Then he remembered that he would not be able to trail the poet that night because he would have to hurry home. It would be too obvious if he came home very late—not only obvious, but also dangerous. Dangerous for many reasons, of which one especially was convincing and unpleasant: there were times when his father would take off his heavy brown belt. Not even in such great moments as these could Koko afford to forget that.

"We're going," said Mario suddenly, leaping from the armchair. "We're going, little one! I can't wait until tomorrow."

And in the twinkling of an eye, the long-haired poet rushed to the window and climbed the window sill, and the scraping, panting, and rumbling began all over again. It seemed as though the whole corner of the house would collapse.

Koko waited until everything was completely still. Then he cautiously moved the armchair and smiled with satisfaction when he observed that the unlucky gray animal was no longer there. Evidently he had gone with his master.

When he finally touched the ground—descending slowly, the same way as the poet had—he began to run toward his own house. The complete silence clearly indicated the late hour of the night. Though he worried about how he was going to face his parents, still he could not help reflecting on his great discovery.

"The camera and Cockroach's picture taking, all of that won't be needed now. Finally everything is clear. The question is whether they are going to strike at the Leibs' tonight. Maybe they will! Well, well, who would have thought it? But why not? It's not so strange. His appearance, his build! He's tall and might seem slightly hunchbacked! Oh, why couldn't I have guessed that he was the tall figure I saw the night before last at the Tonchiches'. Now all I have to do is to prove it! If only I can catch them in the deed! Perhaps we'll be able to tomorrow. Tomorrow, tomorrow!"

17

Face to Face

In the Leib house the evening was passing as usual, peaceful and calm. Milan, who was engaged to Cockroach's sister, had come unexpectedly from the garrison and had taken his fiancée to town. He had promised to talk with his commanding officer about the thieves on Green Hill. He could not say anything for certain, but he hoped that by the following week the army could post some guards here until the militia were in a position to help. Naturally this encouraged and gladdened Margaret Leib, who was afraid that their house would also be robbed. And old Rudolf became quite good-humored, happy that his cool unconcern was really justified. In the first place, nothing of his had been stolen as yet, and it now seemed as though the thieves would meet their end by next week.

"I told you"—he addressed his smiling wife—"that they wouldn't dare come here. There's the revolver and that high wall topped with glass, and . . ." Not knowing what else to add, he stared at the end of his cane, which was leaning against the chair. ". . . and . . . now they'll soon hear about the military guard. Then we'll be through with the thieves. I tell you, the war is over."

"Well," said Margaret, smiling, for she was still rather unconvinced, "from what Milan says, it seems to me that the army will not be here before next Thursday or Friday. A lot can still happen in seven days!"

"Come now, come now. You must have read too many adventure stories in your youth!" Rudolf laughed and reached for the newspapers on the table.

To Cockroach's surprise, the evening went by quite fast. Luckily he came to supper just on time, so that he was not scolded or questioned. He was convinced that Koko had succeeded in making his getaway in time. Most important of all, the camera was in his room, underneath the wardrobe. Now everything was ready.

His father was tired or—what was far more important—he could find nothing interesting in the newspapers, so he soon decided to go to bed. His mother followed suit, and both went up the stairs together. The boy kissed his parents, wished them good night, and said that he would stay downstairs only about ten minutes more, until he finished reading an interesting book about South Sea pirates that Milan had brought him. There were only a few more pages left.

To be sure, as soon as he heard his parents enter their bedroom, he set the book aside. He had to be quick. Luckily, his sister would sleep in town, with an aunt, so there was no need to wait for her. That is, he did not have to be afraid that she would show up and spoil everything. Hastily he took off his sandals, peeled off his socks, and approached the window. The window did not creak at all and opened easily. He leaped into the garden, glanced at the lighted window of the bedroom, and ran to the gate. There he took a key out of his pocket, unlocked the gate, opened it as softly as he could, and ran around the house. With another smaller key he opened the lock on the door to the chicken house. Then he ran to the house.

He climbed back through the window, lowered it carefully, shut the book, turned off the light, and began to climb the stairs. He hurried so that his parents might not suspect anything, and he even stamped hard with his feet that they might hear him going to bed.

Once in his room, he did not turn on the light but went

to the open window and stared out into the night. It was quite clear, and the moonlight was fairly bright. A light breeze rustled in the branches of the fruit trees and the pines. Now he would wait.

Cockroach realized how dangerous and uncertain this whole venture was. First of all, it meant an unpleasant surprise for his mother, who would wail over the stolen chickens, and then she probably would not be able to sleep a single night after that from fear. Besides, it was a question whether the thieves would come tonight at all. And who could tell whether he would succeed in leaving the gate and the chicken house open the following nights. By tomorrow his sister would surely be at home, and then everything would be much more difficult. Finally, it was a big question whether the pictures would turn out well and whether the militia would be able to make use of them. However, Cockroach took comfort in the fact that things of this sort were constantly happening in the funny papers and in stories; the police already had a whole collection of photographs of suspicious persons, and it would be simple to compare them with the new pictures. Sometimes even the smallest detail was sufficient to catch a big criminal. These last thoughts encouraged Cockroach, and now there was only one thing that troubled him and against which he had to struggle: drowsiness. He no longer believed in the myth about black coffee. On the contrary, he was convinced of the opposite. That is why he now relied completely on his own will power. He tried with all his might to keep his eyelids open; he rubbed his eyes with his fists and shook his head. He knew that he would never forgive himself if he fell asleep tonight. This was no longer child's play. The success of the whole venture depended on him. He would not dare face his friends without the pictures.

The moon seemed to wink slyly. Whenever Cockroach turned toward the dark interior of the room, he would hear

the ticking of the old clock, which he was trying not to hear.
The big fish eyes in the picture on the wall watched him
carefully with their gleaming white pupils.

"A-ha, a-ha, a-ha . . ." ticked the tireless clock. It occurred to Cockroach that he might be able to make use of it,
so he tiptoed to the other end of the room and stared at the
strange Roman numerals on its face to keep from falling
asleep. It was close to eleven o'clock. Just then Koko was
getting out of his unpleasant scrape and was climbing down
the rain pipe. Of course, Cockroach knew nothing about all
that. He was waiting, holding the camera in his hand. He
was as impatient as a hunter lying in wait. But, of course, he
was much sleepier.

No sooner did the clock strike eleven than something
creaked in the yard. At that moment Cockroach was trying
to keep his eyelids open with his fingers. In the twinkling of
an eye he was wide awake. He was not mistaken: the creaking came from the big iron gate he had unlocked. He grew
alarmed that his parents might wake up. That would spoil
everything. He was almost angry with the thieves for being
so awkward. However, it was almost as if they did not care
whether anyone heard them that night or not. In fact, that
night they didn't seem to care at all. Their behavior was
strange. To be more exact, *his* behavior, since only one hu-
man form slipped through the gate.

It was a rather small man, thin and agile.

"That's him!" the lad on the second floor thought. "That's
the one we're looking for. Now I'll get him . . ."

He was about to point the camera at the thief when his
attention was attracted by something else. The unknown
prowler had a big handkerchief across his mouth, and he
wore a black mask over his eyes. In his hand there glistened
a long knife! He was exactly as Cockroach had pictured him.
Only somehow he could not believe that this man was from
their part of the country. "Around here no one knows how

to dress for such things. This must be a real thief, just like in the funny papers. If I only knew in which pocket he carries his gun! Probably in the right back pocket."

It was time to get on with the picture taking. The thief caught sight of the stable and went toward it. On the stable door were thick bolts and locks. He looked them over carefully, completely lighted by the moon. Cockroach aimed the camera, waited for his hand to stop trembling, and snapped the shutter. Then something happened that he did not expect at all. The unknown prowler with the black mask must have heard the quiet, sharp click. This was not particularly strange; indeed, Cockroach had half expected this. However, what happened then exceeded all his expectations. The thief reached for his right hip pocket, and in his hand there flashed a revolver. He pointed it straight at the window at which Cockroach was standing with the camera.

Cockroach dropped to the floor like lightning. No shot was heard. Evidently the thief did not fire. Quickly the boy felt his face, forehead, and chest to see if he had been wounded anywhere. He was afraid that in the excitement he might have missed hearing the shot.

"A-ha, a-ha, a-ha." The clock laughed in the corner.

Feeling the sweat on his face and the wobbliness in his knees, Cockroach tried after several minutes to sit up and look through the curtains to see what was going on in the yard. "They might kill me! What then? But even that is better than to act like a coward. Besides . . . there is a question whether he could hit me or not."

When he finally straightened up, he lifted the camera again and looked through the curtains. A little cloud clung to the moon, so that it was dark outside. He had to push the curtains aside. He kept still and listened to the loud beating of his heart:

"Ta-taa, ta-taaa, ta-taaa."

"A-ha, a-ha, a-ha," the tireless clock sounded forth.

Cockroach peered between the curtains. When the cloud passed, he cautiously moved forward so that he might see the whole garden and yard.

He immediately spied the armed robber. He was standing in front of the chicken house, with his back turned and bending over. Then something clanked, creaked, and crunched. The lock had closed! The question was whether the thief had done it on purpose. In that case, he must have been very clumsy, and the boy with the camera could not believe that. Be that as it may, the chicken house was now locked, and all the chickens were safe and sound. Cockroach took one more picture, from the back, and the unknown prowler heard nothing this time.

Then something else happened that confused the boy on the second floor—something that was perhaps not entirely meaningless, something that perhaps indicated the nocturnal visitor had not shut the lock accidentally, something that perhaps showed that on that particular night the thieves were not at all interested in stealing.

The rather small man with the mask once more reached for his pocket, and Cockroach, who was about to fall to the floor again, saw that instead of a weapon he produced a piece of paper. Then the thief drew a knife from his belt and used it to nail the sheet of paper to the door of the chicken house! Finally, pausing several paces away from the gate, he cast a hasty glance, first at the posted sheet of paper, and then at the window where the green-eyed lad was standing. Their eyes met for a moment, and Cockroach saw the unknown prowler's eyes glisten behind the slits of the mask. There was a chance to snap a third picture, but he did not think of it at the time. The next moment the mysterious visitor disappeared through the garden gate. Moreover, he carefully closed it behind him!

Cockroach stared wide-eyed at the prominent sheet of paper and the gleam of the knife blade. He had no doubt that it was a message. He was only afraid that it might be a trap. Therefore, he waited a while longer. He was completely awake now, and his ear caught every sound. Nothing could be heard.

After a half hour—maybe it was a bit more, maybe less— he decided to go down into the yard, no matter what happened. What would he discover in the mysterious message?

Carefully he opened the door and stole through the corridor. He ran down the stairs hastily on the tips of his bare toes.

18

The Skull and Crossbones

Tom was sleeping especially soundly. True, he had fallen asleep with some difficulty, since he was quite angry with himself. Blacky and Bozo had scolded him severely for not finding out anything at Emmie's. As a matter of fact, they had not scolded him nearly as much as he had himself for having blabbed everything. His only comfort was the knowledge that Emmie was good-natured and reliable and that she would surely not tell anyone. However, all these thoughts tortured him until late at night, so that he fell asleep completely exhausted. For this reason his slumber was unusually deep. And in the morning, of course, he did not get up as early as usual. The sun was already quite high, but he slept on, curled up like a pretzel. It was past nine.

When a stubborn ray of sun finally shone on his forehead, eyelids, and cheeks, he opened first one eye and then the other. The light hindered his sight. The window and the balcony door were open, and a fresh breeze was playing with the curtains and with a feather that had escaped from the pillow and was wafting about in the air.

Each morning Tom awoke with the same thought: "Were we robbed last night?" He would listen for a long time until he heard his mother's measured footsteps in the kitchen and the loud conversation of his father in the barbershop. Then he would conclude: "No, everything is all right. Nothing has happened." If something had happened, he would have considered himself to blame, because he had not remained

awake for the fateful moment. Today it was very busy in the
lower part of the house, which meant that there were already many visitors in the barbershop and that it must be
fairly late. Tom reflected that last night Cockroach had
probably completed his assignment, and that made him
happy. When he went to town to take the film to be developed, he would call to him through the window as he
had promised. Only, what if he had already passed by?

Tom briskly rubbed his eyes with his fists, sat up in bed,
and threw back the covers. Before getting up, he glanced at
his legs—to see whether it was necessary to wash them that
morning. His glance stopped at the lower end of the bed:
a sheet of paper was affixed to the wood. It was stuck there
by a long straight pin with a black head. Moreover, it was

apparent that something was written on the paper and that at the bottom there was some kind of sign.

The lad flopped over in bed like a fish so that his feet came to rest where his head had been and his head was at the opposite end. With bulging eyes and gaping mouth, he read to himself the unusual message, which was scrawled in thick letters:

> LITTLE FOOL!
>   LAY OFF THE KID STUFF AND DON'T STICK YOUR NOSE INTO EVERYTHING, OR ELSE. . . . THE SAME GOES FOR YOUR FRIENDS.

Instead of a signature, a large skull and crossbones was drawn clumsily beneath the letters.

At first Tom lay as stiff as a mummy, and then he shook himself. Hastily he withdrew the straight pin from the wood, threw it out the window, and clasped the paper in his fist. He got up, put on his pants, and stuffed the sheet of paper into his pocket, after folding it twice. He then stood in the middle of the room, not knowing what to do next. Thoughts buzzed around his head like pesky flies. "Who did it? How could he have come here? If Mama did not notice, that means that *somebody* has been here this morning, just a short while ago! Had the others also received warnings?" He finally realized that nothing could come of such empty suppositions. He had to meet with the others as soon as possible.

He rushed down the stairs and went into the kitchen.

"G'morning," he said carelessly.

"Good morning," his mother replied. "You certainly got up early! Your breakfast is over there on the table."

Tom did not like breakfast much anyway, and he would have felt especially lucky to be able to skip it today. Nevertheless, not to make his mother angry, he obediently sat at the table. He watched his mother. Had she noticed the piece of paper on his bed? Judging by everything, no. She would have already asked about it, or else she would have taken it off herself. "Anyway," he recalled, licking the honey off the bread that his mother had just spread and placed on a plate beside him, "they probably know that Mother gets up early and that I am left alone in the room." He was possessed with pride that they, the thieves, the criminals, had to take account of him. However, a lot of hidden terror was mixed into that pride.

"Look at you!" His mother suddenly spoke, and Tom quickly snapped out of his reverie. "Eat the bread, too, and don't just lick off the honey!"

He bit into the bread. At the same time he secretly slipped the folded piece of paper from his pocket, spread it under the table, and examined it thoroughly once more. Two things about it bothered him especially. In the first place, it called him a little fool, and then it had that unpleasant drawing at the bottom that smacked of real danger.

Outside a whistle pierced the air: one short, then one long. That was Cockroach, who was going to town.

Tom gulped down the rest of his breakfast and sped out of the house. He placed his hand over his eyes to shield them from the sun and spied his friend, who was leaning against the fence, happily whistling and trying to dig out a clump of grass with his foot.

It was not a time for ordinary greetings. Tom asked him immediately, "Well?" But he did not wait for an answer to this vague query. Rather he glanced fearfully toward the house and drew out of his pocket the message with the skull and crossbones. "Read," he uttered in a shaky voice.

Cockroach looked in astonishment at his friend, then at the piece of paper, unfolded it, and read it. An odd smile flitted over his face. He also dug into his pocket and took out a large sheet of paper that had been pierced through the middle by a sharp object.

"You read this!" he said significantly, and again began to gouge the grass with his foot.

Tom carefully reached for the paper as though afraid it would explode in his hand, and he read it, trying to keep his hands from trembling:

> LITTLE SQUIRT!
>
> DO YOU THINK THAT I AM AFRAID OF YOU AND THE OTHER FOOLS? OR THAT I AM AFRAID BECAUSE OF THE CAMERA YOU STOLE? I KNOW WHO YOU ARE, BUT YOU DON'T KNOW WHO I AM! LAY OFF THE KID STUFF OR YOU'LL GET HURT. THIS IS THE FIRST AND LAST WARNING.
>
> DON'T STICK YOUR NOSE WHERE IT DOESN'T BELONG. WASN'T IT CHILDISH TO TAKE THE LOCK OFF THE GATE? I SHALL COME WHEN YOU AREN'T EXPECTING ME!

The handwriting was the same as in the first note, and instead of a signature here too was a skull and crossbones. Tom was dumfounded, but at the same time he was also somehow glad, first of all because they were not after just him, and then because he was not the only one they called a little fool.

"And did you get a look at them? Did you take their picture?" he finally remembered to ask.

"I saw him. Actually there was only one of them. Strangest of all, he did not take anything, even though I left the door of the chicken house open."

"And you saw him! What's he like?"

"Rather short, thin. Wears a mask. He looks like that crazy poet whose camera we took. Besides, he saw me and chased me away from the window with his gun. And where did you find your note?"

"On the bed! He must have climbed up the balcony. This is somebody who knows everything."

"No doubt about it!" said Cockroach, and again laughed knowingly. "He even knew that I was going to photograph him."

"Do you think there is only one of them?"

"No, I don't think so. There are certainly at least two of them! They only want to lead us off the track with these letters, writing as though only one man did it. Besides, naturally he hopes that we shall become frightened. That is why he added the sign of the Phantom."

"What kind of sign?" Tom was startled and gaped open-mouthed.

"Phantom, I said. That's from the funnypapers. The Phantom is a man with a black mask, and he has a seal on his ring. When he hits somebody, the sign of the skull and crossbones remains on his skin. They figure that we read those funny papers and that they can frighten us in this way. But they can't!"

Tom did not understand much of this, but he did not want to show it. Rather he asked, "Are you going to town?"

"Yes, I have to hurry. I wonder how the photos will turn out. And you go over to Koko. We'll meet there. And don't talk too much. Say only that both of us received warnings and show yours. You can say that I was able to take the pictures and that I went to town to have the snapshots developed."

"All right. What else could I say anyway?"

"Don't mention that I saw the gun, that he left me his knife, and so on. Don't tell what you read in the message to me."

"Why? Why not?" Tom asked.

"What do you think?" Cockroach inquired instead of answering, as he dug with his foot and carefully observed the grass as though it was terribly important. "How could these thieves know about our every move if only we know? Huh?"

Tom stared in amazement and gasped, "I . . . I don't know."

Then Cockroach, who was on the point of leaving, added even more remarkable words.

"Don't be afraid. I don't think it's you . . . but one of us must be a traitor, isn't it so?" Here he gave his younger friend a tap on the shoulder. "Come on, come on, don't wonder so much. It happens! Just go over to Koko and tell him what I told you. I'll come back soon. So long!"

And he hurried down the road toward town, while Tom remained motionless in front of his house, staring somewhere into space over the endless stretch of plowland to the south. He had not even gathered his wits sufficiently to reply to his friend's farewell.

19

Another Letter

Blacky went to open the door. His worst weeks were those in which his mother worked the night shift. Then he had to get up early in the morning to take the milk from the milkman, for his mother did not get back until eight o'clock. Above all, his little five-year-old brother usually woke up, and there was no end to his yelling until Blacky warmed his milk or else picked a handful of fruit from someone else's orchard.

"All right, all right!" he impatiently answered the milkman, who was pounding on the door with his fist and who, naturally, woke up little Drago.

The milkman spilled some of the milk on the floor beside the pan as he poured it from a huge blue can. Also he was unusually talkative, and it was hard to get rid of him. On this particular morning Blacky had decided not to talk at all so that the conversation would soon dry up. Nevertheless, before he left, the milkman pointed toward the yard gate and announced:

"I think you have a letter at the gate. Maybe it was left over from yesterday. Someone must have come. Sometimes one doesn't notice. I know once my godfather came, all the way from town, imagine—that's quite a distance—and the man happened to come just when I wasn't at home. And when he saw that I wasn't at home . . ."

"Thank you, all right," said Blacky, and spat out the door.

Blacky went back into the house, quieted little Drago, who was trying to fall on his head from the high bed, placed the milk on the stove, and lighted the fire. Then he remembered the letter, looked outside to make sure the milkman had finally left, and went out into the yard.

A blue envelope was fastened to the green wooden gate by a straight pin. It bore no address but only a single word in thick letters: BLACKY. He was unable even to guess what it was all about. He spat through his teeth, almost as far as the other side of the road, and went back into the house. Taking a knife from the table, he carefully opened the envelope at one end. Beneath his fingers he could feel two little sheets of paper, and he drew them out. One was a blue sheet that went with the envelope, and the other was a somewhat larger single sheet of plain white paper. It was not quite daylight, and Blacky went out of the house again in order to be able to read both notes more easily.

At first his face showed displeasure, then great wonderment and surprise, and finally something akin to satisfaction. His black eyebrows, which were usually one right up against the other, separated a bit in the middle. Again he spat far, clicked his tongue, and snapped his fingers. His mouth spread in a wide smile. Then he began to whistle merrily.

With his foot he opened the door of the house. He knew by the smell in the kitchen that the milk had boiled over. Besides, his little brother had finally succeeded in falling on his head and now was sitting on the floor, his mouth wide open, and crying with all his might. But none of this bothered the older brother this time. He calmly took off the remaining milk, wiped the stove with a wet rag, and went to the child. He was very gentle, so that Drago quickly grew quiet. He only sighed loudly and sniffled from time to time.

Blacky drank his own milk and gave another cup to his little brother. Then he again drew out the blue envelope from his pocket, took out the white sheet of paper, and carried it to his bed. He bent over and stuck it between the springs. He folded the other sheet carefully, smoothed it out with the palm of his hand, and placed it in the back pocket of his trousers. He went to the table, opened the drawer, and looked at the old-fashioned watch of his dead father. His mother would soon be back. He rubbed his hands and sat in his chair again.

But he simply could not sit still. He stood up again in a minute and began to pace around the room, not knowing what to do with his hands. He was unusually excited. Even little Drago, who was sitting on the floor with mouth and eyes wide open, carefully watched his brother's strange behavior.

The sun had already risen, and its slanting rays lighted the interior of the little bungalow on the northern slope of Green Hill. It was the beginning of a new day.

20

Even Those Who Have Nothing Have Hope

Naturally, one cannot think of everything. It always happens that a man forgets to do something that is vitally important—especially if he does not know that he ought to do it. Such was Cockroach's experience. Up to that day it had seemed to him that photography was very simple and that he knew all about it. However, apparently there were certain little things he did not know about and that were, judging by everything, of great importance. Especially if one takes pictures at night.

Anyway, the photographer took the film and went into his darkroom. When he returned, he said that the last three pictures had not turned out at all. Cockroach went out of the shop with his head low.

He hardly noticed the town around him. The streetcars had been put back into operation, and the bustle of the city again filled the streets. On a field between some ruined houses children were playing with a real honest-to-goodness leather football. But the black-haired boy with the green eyes did not want to look at anything. In his troubled state of mind he probably would not have seen very much anyway. It seemed to him that everything was finished. Of course, he was not to blame that he was returning with empty hands. Nevertheless, he would rather have had this happen to someone else. Now there was no sense in trying anything more. What he had told Tom about a traitor in their ranks was bare suspicion, nonsense. He had not really believed it and had said it only to impress his friend. But now, even if it was true, there was nothing else to do anyway.

In the darkest possible mood, Cockroach passed through the outskirts of town and came out on Green Hill Road. He was also furious because his parents had not permitted him to go to town on the bicycle. He stopped the first peasant cart that came along and asked for a ride. The good-natured old man, who was as wrinkled as a prune and as straight as a candle, agreed to take him, so the boy clambered up on a heap of pumpkins. He wanted to get to Koko's as soon as possible to report to his friends and then to go somewhere far, far away. He wished fervently to lie down in a meadow, in the shade of an old oak, and to sleep through at least several days. The cart stopped where the road branched off for the neighboring village. After a brief thanks, the lad hurried off to the next fork in the road and then took Lake Road.

Even from a distance he could see that his friends were gathered in the Milich yard. There was Bozo, Tom, Blacky, and, of course, the host Koko, who seemed to be especially excited. As usual, Blacky was sitting a bit apart from the rest, on a log. He was even more serious and thoughtful than usual.

As soon as Cockroach entered the yard, Bozo immediately greeted him with the question: "Did you hear whether anyone was robbed last night?"

"No, I didn't hear anything," the newcomer mumbled gruffly, and angrily thought to himself, "He could at least have asked about the pictures. After all, I risked my life for them!"

"Tom says that you were able to take the pictures," Koko remembered to ask, and then added mysteriously, "even though that's not important now."

"Yes, I snapped his picture, but the picture didn't turn out. For night shots one needs a flash."

"What?" Tom was amazed.

"A flash," Cockroach repeated, as though it were all very obvious. "For light."

"That means, nothing doing?" Koko asked rather cheerfully. "But . . ."

"Wait!" Bozo interrupted again and turned to the inept photographer. "You also received a message, didn't you? What does yours say?"

"Did you all get one too?" Cockroach inquired, and he took out of his pocket the pierced sheet of paper and gave it to the lad with the glasses. Then, remembering his recent suspicions, he cautiously added, "Is there anyone perhaps who didn't get one?"

Tom realized what was behind this question, so he curiously observed all present. However, there was no point to the suspicion; all had received similar threatening and insulting warnings. Therefore, it seemed, no one was in league with the enemy. Unfortunately, it was all the same now. At least, that was what Cockroach thought. But his friends soon convinced him that further action should be taken.

"We know who the thief is!" Tom suddenly blurted out. Blacky looked at him so seriously that he grew numb with shame, and his hands remained motionless in the air, like those of a stone saint giving his blessing.

"What do you know?" Cockroach exclaimed stupefied, and leaned forward as though he was about to fight with someone.

"Sshhh!" Bozo hissed.

"Let's go into the garden. We can talk there."

The boys went toward the garden and the orchard that lay behind the Milich house. As they were passing the door, Koko's mother appeared and called to her son:

"Be careful; don't go away anywhere! Or you'll be in for it when your father comes home!"

Koko said nothing in reply but calmly opened the garden gate and, like a real host, let his friends go in first. A pleasant, fresh coolness pervaded the orchard. It was difficult to imagine a more appropriate place for a secret talk.

They sat near a little mound on which stood a big, uneven board. On it there was scrawled in black clumsy letters:

GIPSEE DIED AWGUST SIXTH

Tom gazed sadly at the humble monument, while Blacky spat, aiming at a nearby plum tree. The boys sat down on the thick grass, except for Koko, who was holding the seat of his pants with an incredibly pained expression. Apparently his mother had done well to remind him not to go away from the house, for such were his father's orders. Last night, when he had come home so late, his father had meant business.

"Well?" Cockroach began impatiently, having just sat down. A new feeling of hope welled up within him.

"The thief is . . ." Tom rushed on, but he felt the reproachful glances of the other boys and kept still, placing his hand over his mouth.

"Wait, Cockroach," said Bozo, settling himself on the ground. "We'll see whether your story tallies with what Koko says. You saw the thief last night, didn't you?"

"Is he short, thin, long-haired?" Koko asked immediately, without waiting for Cockroach's answer.

"Yes, he is thin and on the short side," Cockroach replied slowly, trying to remember the nocturnal apparition, "and as for the hair, I don't know. He wore a cap and a mask, so that it couldn't be seen."

"Well, then," Koko continued in an even happier voice, "you say that he is short and thin. And he has a tomcat with him?"

"Dumbbells!" said Blacky, who was sprawled out in the tall grass so that only his knees could be seen. "Didn't you claim the same thing about Isaac? Wasn't everything then also 'quite clear'? Wise guys!" He fell silent, as though he remembered something. He kept still and spat angrily.

For a while silence reigned, until Cockroach, who concluded that there was no use paying any attention to their tall and somewhat stubborn friend, decided to ask further:

"All right, who is it then?" At this moment he completely forgot that he had half believed that one of them was working for the unknown thief. He was again all for his friends, and he was ready to do anything to ensure the successful completion of their great undertaking. His eyes were bright, and his lower lip stuck out with impatience. "Who is it, huh?"

"Mario, the poet!" Tom blurted out, unable to stand it any longer.

However, no one was angry. It was time to tell Cockroach anyway. They certainly were not going to keep it a secret from him. Naturally, they had wanted to wait a while before making the revelation so that it would be as effective as possible. However, the impression was great enough as it was.

"Mario . . . no . . . no, it isn't possible . . ." Cockroach could not find words. "But . . . how do you know?"

Koko briefly related his experience and the poet's conversation with the tomcat. He would have trailed him had he not been in a hurry to get home. If he had known that his haste would be in vain, he would have gone after the thief and his awful gray animal regardless.

"And you say that he is practicing climbing up rain pipes to make it easier for him to get into people's homes?"

"No doubt about it!"

"He's no longer satisfied with just chickens," added Bozo, who had taken off his glasses meanwhile and was wiping them on his shirt. "Now he wants money, too, cash!"

They explained to Cockroach how they had already agreed to stand guard that evening around the poet's house and to trail him if he went prowling.

Then suddenly Cockroach hit himself on the forehead and, lowering his voice, asked, "How does he know about us? Who told him? And when did he distribute all those warning messages unless he took them with him even when you were in his house?"

"I don't know," Koko wondered, but soon he too hit himself on the forehead. "Of course, I saw . . . that is, I heard him writing something. I was behind the armchair, and, naturally, I couldn't see anything. I thought that he was writing poems. Oh, am I a dope! I could have looked at the sheets of paper. There they were on the floor and on the armchair."

"He probably stuck them in his pocket, and you couldn't see that," Bozo concluded, hiking up his glasses.

It seemed as though there could no longer be any doubt. The long-haired poet must be the thief. The only wonder was that they had not thought of it before. How else could he make a living? Certainly not from his poems!

"But how does he know about us? How does he know that we are trying to catch him and his partner?" stubborn Cockroach continued to ask.

When they shrugged their shoulders, he went on, "Has any one of us blabbed?"

All shook their heads, while Tom did not dare lift his eyes from the tips of his shoes.

"Maybe they are trailing us too!" said Koko carelessly, as though he himself did not believe in that possibility.

"I am sure of that!" Bozo spoke up again. "That's why we must hurry! There's no use in just babbling and guessing."

Soon it was agreed that Cockroach and Bozo would carry out this new, most recent assignment. Blacky could not take part because his mother was working at night and he had to watch his little brother, while Koko did not dare move out of the house because his father would not let him. Nobody even thought of Tom, and he somehow did not seem to take offense. It was as though he had a feeling that his turn was yet to come.

Following Blacky's observation that there was no need to return the camera as yet, since it was probably stolen in the first place, the boys decided to break up the meeting and to return to the same spot the next morning. It was better for them not to be seen together, for their plans were known as it was. Blacky had one more suggestion: to burn the warning messages with the skulls and crossbones as proof that no one was afraid of these threats. Immediately he brought out a box of matches, and soon little bits of charred paper were flying through the air. Only Tom turned his head away in order not to look again at those terrifying signs with the crossbones.

21

Pots Fall from the Skies

That evening the light shone very early from the window of the poet's house. Apparently he was impatient and could hardly wait for night to fall. Two boys, one of whom watched with double eyes, were sitting almost motionless under a fruit tree some twenty yards from the house.

"Do you see the rain pipe?" Cockroach said in a barely audible whisper, for he felt it necessary to explain the whole layout to his friend.

"I see," Bozo mumbled gruffly, irked, first of all, because he could not see the rain pipe, and second, because his older friend was acting so superior. As if he, Bozo, had not already been in a similar situation, when, during that night before the beginning of the storm, he trailed the old man and the dog through the dark forest full of gnarled shadows and the ghostly voices of night birds. To be sure, all of that had been in vain, but it was nonetheless dangerous. Nor could Bozo forget the gleaming sharpness of the knife the old man had been sharpening that morning. There was no reason for Cockroach to act so important.

"Don't talk so much," Bozo finally grunted. "They might hear us."

Meanwhile, the long-haired poet was standing before the mirror, turning on his heels and looking at himself with satisfaction. The tomcat was rubbing against his legs and gazing upon his master with attention and approval.

"What do you say, little one? How does it look to you? Am I not a fine figure of a man, hm?"

The tomcat said nothing in reply but merely tried to rub even harder against the poet's legs.

"Shall we take along the mask?" he asked, as though he really expected a reply. How the boys would have rejoiced had they been able to hear this question! "What do you think? Would it be a good idea or not?"

Naturally, the gray animal said nothing in return but miaowed plaintively. It was apparent that he, too, was impatient.

The poet opened a drawer in the lower part of the wardrobe and took out a black mask. In a trice he put it on, looked again in the mirror, and smiled with satisfaction, his gold teeth gleaming in the artificial light. Then he thrust it into his coat pocket, smoothed down his shirt, and winked at the tomcat.

The animal miaowed once more and raised its proud tail in a question mark.

Mario turned out the light and approached the window, perhaps planning to slide down the rain pipe. But he changed his mind and said, "No, there's no point to it. I will get dirty enough as it is. Let's go, little one, through the door."

The lads lying in ambush crouched down and stretched out a leg, ready to go. They were a bit surprised when the poet did not leave by way of the window, but they pulled themselves together when they saw him descending the stairs and going into the yard.

"Perhaps somebody warned him that we are here!" Cockroach whispered again, remembering his dark suspicions of that morning.

"Shut up!" the shortsighted lad snapped. "Look!"

Mario had gone around the corner of the house and was scanning the sky. Then he looked down at his feet. His faithful tomcat was at his side. Finally, he set out toward the

little path that led directly to the highest point of Green
Hill, from which one could view the entire countryside.

"He's the one!" Cockroach could not help gasping. "At
first he seemed taller than the one I saw last night, but I
see now that they are the same height. Even their move-
ments are the same."

His taciturn friend only gave him a furious glance from
behind his murky, thick glasses. Both stood up and started
after the poet.

"Tomcats surely can't smell as well as dogs," Bozo thought.
"I think it doesn't matter which side the wind is blowing
from."

Meanwhile, Mario did not take the little path but struck
out directly across it and began to descend southward across
the bare fields. After about ten paces he again looked
around carefully, crouched a little, and turned left, uphill.
Soon he changed his course again and entered the little
woods that bordered on the orchards of the Radiches and
Lucy Bobich.

"He is going to the Radiches!" Cockroach gasped. He was
so overcome by the course of events that he almost lost sight
of the need for caution.

"Ssshhh!" Bozo hissed and added softly, brusquely, "To
Lucy's!"

Both of them looked around carefully. It was quite unpleasant to think that perhaps somebody was on their heels
too. Cockroach did not wish to admit that he had brought
along the knife that the mysterious visitor of last night had
so readily presented to him by using it to stick the note to
the door. He kept still, pressing it in his damp hand.

The man and the cat stopped where the wood touched on
the two fenced-in orchards.

"Now he'll turn left," Cockroach predicted.

"To the right," Bozo thought.

The poet climbed the fence, tottered for a moment as

though he would fall, straightened up, and landed in the right orchard after all.

"He is going to Lucy's!" the older boy exclaimed in consternation and disappointment.

"He must think that she has money," Bozo said calmly, trying by his tone of voice to convey that everything was turning out exactly as he had expected.

Without losing a second, the boys jumped over the fence, making scarcely any noise at all. The rows of fruit trees were fairly far apart from one another, so that they could spy on Mario and his four-legged favorite from a distance. Indeed, the poet was going straight toward the house. Light showed from only one window: the highest one.

"Little one," the long-haired man whispered, pressing his hand against his heart. "Little one, the time has come. Only let me catch my breath." He leaned against a nearby pear tree and tried to breathe more calmly. Realizing that they had to rest, the tomcat sat down and began to lick his front paws, which had been muddied by the wet ground. By now the boys were only about twenty paces behind them.

Through the lighted window there floated a song. All four of them glanced up in the hope of seeing the woman who was singing in a pleasant voice. But the song suddenly ended, and the light went out. The poet straightened up and, with a motion of his hand, showed the tomcat that he must not follow him farther. The animal did not show that it was either saddened or offended. It was as though it expected just that.

The boys nudged each other in the ribs with their elbows. The robber-poet was placing a black mask over his face!

"This is it!" Bozo exulted.

"Just the same, he seemed shorter to me last night," Cockroach pondered, "probably because I was looking from above." Then he exclaimed involuntarily, "Oh! There he is by the rain pipe!"

Indeed, along the northern wall there rose a wide rain pipe, exactly like the one on the poet's house. It passed right next to the window that had been lighted up a moment ago. Finally everything was clear. The sly thief had been practicing on his own rain pipe to make it easier for him to climb into other people's houses later. He had already stolen practically everything that people had left in their yards, and now he had decided to try to break into their houses as well. It was no wonder that he intended to rob a lonely woman first! There was still one puzzle. Cockroach asked softly:

"I'd like to know where that partner of his is!"

"Partner? Who says that he has a partner anyway?"

"But Koko saw two of them. At the Tonchiches'."

"Koko! Koko!" Bozo shook his head. "Koko is a well-known liar. Besides, he was so afraid that he might have seen double."

Cockroach was dumfounded at his younger friend's unexpected seriousness. He had spoken in such a convincing tone that it was impossible not to believe in his words. Of course, why should they believe Koko?

Meanwhile, there was not much time for thinking, since Mario was about to climb the rain pipe. He stroked it with his hand and looked around carefully. Then he smoothed down his hair with the palms of his hands once more and placed his foot on the first joint. An arduous ascent began. Three pairs of curious eyes watched him carefully out of the darkness.

He stopped halfway to wipe his face with his coat sleeve, while hanging on by his other arm. He finally made another effort. And then another. The window was no longer so far away.

"What shall we do when he goes inside?" Bozo asked suddenly, happening to remember that they had not discussed at all just how they would catch or unmask the bold thief.

"We'll call out, we'll shout. Just let him go in, the skunk."

But Bozo, who was showing more and more his capability and sharp-mindedness that evening, triumphantly whispered: "We'll break off the lower end of the rain pipe. I think it can be done. We'll cut off his escape. Meanwhile we can shout, too. He won't get away . . ."

They were not able to finish discussing their ideas. At that very moment events began to unfold rapidly. The disheveled poet was already within reach of the window, and just as the boys expected him to break into the house, he said something half aloud. They could not understand what he said, nor would it have helped them much if they had, inasmuch as the words were poetic. As a matter of fact, the poet recited the following at the open window: "Lucy, behold thy humble troubadour, who comes to thee with a new poem!" Then he reached for his pocket, while dangerously dangling in the air, and with his left hand he drew out a sheet of paper. Apparently he did not have to read it. He knew his verses by heart:

> "In the forest deep
> My love doth sleep;
> Hither I creep
> And my vigil keep,
> As my heart doth weep . . ."

Anyway, the words themselves did not matter much. More important was how they were received. At first, for a few moments, an unbroken silence reigned in the dark house. Then suddenly a shrill female voice cried out, the same that had sung so prettily just a while ago, only now it was no longer tender. The light came on, and Lucy appeared at the window, with rumpled hair and clenched fists. It was clear that she was scolding, though her words could not be fully understood by the boys. "Scribbler! How long will you continue to annoy me? Why did you climb up the rain pipe like an ape! What did you stick over your face? Get lost and

don't let me see you again, or else . . ." And not knowing
what else to do to the unfortunate poet, she reached for a
flowerpot and hurled it at the head with the black mask. It
did not strike its target, since the climber descended to the
ground like an arrow. A rather plump cactus came flying at
him next. Mario ran off without looking around. But he
could not escape the scolding.

"Empty-headed rascal! You annoy those who cannot de-
fend themselves. Do you think that I have to listen to you?
Just you come again, just let me see you once more, you ape
. . . and I'll . . ."

As the poet was approaching with unbelievable speed,
having far outstripped the tomcat, the boys could not hear
all that the fiery widow intended to do to him. They withdrew to one side while the man and the cat sped past them.
Mario did not even take time to remove his mask.

At any other time this event might have seemed funny.
But the boys had no stomach for comedy. Bozo sighed
deeply, while Cockroach slammed a fist into the palm of his
hand. This was the second time they had been on the wrong
track. The real thief, who knew everything about them, was
certainly having a good laugh at their childish mistakes.
They were in no mood to laugh now. They bit their lips
furiously.

22

Sleepwalking

Tom usually slept very well and never woke up until morning. That night, however, his sleep was troubled and restless. Perhaps the reason was that his mother had remained in town to spend the night with a sick aunt and that he was now sleeping alone in the big, half-empty room. Perhaps another reason was that all day there had hovered before his eyes a picture of the terrible unknown prowler with the black mask climbing on the balcony, entering the room, approaching his bed, and cold-bloodedly pinning up a sheet of paper with a skull and crossbones. Deep down in his heart the boy was convinced that Blacky had acted unreasonably in burning all the messages. One never knows in such cases what they might have led to! "Maybe it would have been better had we handed them over to the police," he thought.

Be that as it may, Tom suddenly lay with his eyes wide open. He was almost completely awake. Outside the night was murky, without a moon, which was enveloped in clouds. The whisper of the wind in the leaves was ghostly. It was a time of terror for the boy who was alone in the large room, in the large bed.

Had he heard something in his sleep? He could not remember. Anyway, he was convinced that he had not awakened just by chance. And he was not mistaken. Soon he heard again that which had really awakened him.

Someone was walking. Muffled footsteps and squeaking shoes. The boy slowly raised himself up and tensely began to listen. Someone was walking around in the yard.

Once Tom would not have noticed such a noise. Once he would not have been awakened by these quiet footsteps. But now, when danger hung over him like a sword, he believed that he must investigate what was going on. Perhaps even in his sleep he deemed it his duty to wake up.

In the twinkling of an eye he jumped out of bed. The floor was cold, and an unpleasant breeze covered him with goose-pimples. Carefully he pushed the curtains apart and stepped out on the small balcony. He was scarcely afraid, for he firmly believed that there must be a mistake somewhere. There was nothing in their yard for anyone to steal. Everything had been put away in the house. "Besides," he thought, "besides, Bozo and Cockroach are surely nearby." He did not suspect that his two friends were sitting helplessly in the grass, under the pear trees, and gazing hopelessly in front of them. "If it is that crazy poet, so much the better," he thought further, without really knowing why it was better.

It was not Mario. It was Tom's brother Ivo. Tom sighed with relief and smiled. Somehow he had guessed that it would be Ivo. Who else would walk about the yard at night? As a matter of fact, secretly Tom did not believe in the stories about the thieves. That is, he liked to think that there were some sort of supernatural beings that appeared and disappeared whenever it pleased them. Look at the way they had tricked the boys! Who else could enter into somebody's house in the morning and stick a sheet of paper with a skull and crossbones on a bed? How was it that he heard the footsteps in the yard now, but he could not hear them when they were right next to his bed? Naturally, the boy would not have dared confide his strange ideas about the mysterious invisible beings to anyone. Just the same, sometimes it seemed to him that that was the only possible solution to the mystery of Green Hill.

He was about to turn around and go back into the room

when a strange circumstance attracted his attention. Ivo was completely dressed, which was very odd in view of the time of night. Tom knew that his brother smoked in secret, but he doubted that he would do this at night. Besides, he would hardly dress from head to toe for that. Something was wrong. Tom looked again at the yard. Perhaps Ivo wanted to catch the thieves himself.

Ivo was going in the direction of the fence. Then he stopped as though he was making up his mind and turned off toward the woodshed. There he raised himself up on his toes and slipped an arm under the roof. Something gleamed in his hand: it was a knife! He stuck it in a sheath, which he pulled out of his pocket, and then again inserted his arm in the hole underneath the roof. Tom was amazed; his brother was pushing a real gun into the back pocket of his trousers!

Having thus armed himself, Ivo went toward the gate that let into the garden, opened it, and carefully closed it behind him. Tom hid himself behind the curtain just in time to avoid being seen by his brother, who was looking straight at the balcony. Apparently, he did not notice anything. Otherwise, he would not have walked so coldly and calmly through the garden.

Tom stood behind the curtains a while longer, listening to the loud beating of his own heart. He had already decided that something ought to be done, but he could not pull himself together. He could not grasp the meaning of Ivo's mysterious departure, but he was quite sure there was something behind it. No doubt about it—he had to follow his brother, no matter what happened. He began to wonder how he was going to carry this out. He did not dare think of going through the house. His father would probably wake up, and then everything would end very, very badly. The only clear path led over the balcony. The boy went outside again and looked down: it was quite high. Had it been a matter of showing off in front of somebody, for example in

front of little Emmie, maybe he would have dared jump into that dark abyss; but since he was alone, he quite correctly gauged his own capabilities. He knew that he was fairly awkward and that he would probably come to no good end in such a breakneck jump. Then it occurred to him that he might let himself down by some sort of rope. He gathered up the bedclothes and began to pull off the sheet. He knew that this was the way prisoners escaped from jail. At least in books.

One sheet was too short, so he threw off the pillows and blankets from his mother's bed. He worked as fast as possible, tied both sheets together with a huge knot, and ran out to the balcony again. He tied one end of the sheet rope to the wide railing and looked down with satisfaction. The sheets went almost to the ground.

"Getting back will be

easier," he thought. "There is a ladder behind the woodshed!"

He tested the tightness of the knot he had tied around the railing, ran into the room once more, put on his short pants and shirt, and returned to the balcony. He went over the railing and began to descend the white ribbon. Finally he touched ground. His bare feet did not make a sound.

The main part of the task was still before him. He had to catch up with his brother. Tom ran as fast as his legs could carry him. He entered the garden and began to hop over the heads of cabbage and the pumpkins. Ivo was probably a long way off by now, and what was worse, Tom did not know which direction to take in pursuit. Besides, there was also the danger that he might run right into Ivo.

But luck smiled on him. In the distance glowed a bright red dot. It was the end of a lighted cigarette. Tom slowed down, carefully going around the stakes for the tomato plants. The smoker was already out in the field. Turning left, he went around the Leibs' vineyard and came out on Rocco Road, which formed the northern boundary of Green Hill.

Here and there in the sky, the clouds had been scattered by the breeze and stars winked at the earth. A boy who was already growing a mustache was walking rapidly toward the north. Another smaller boy was cautiously stalking after him, taking advantage of the shadows of lonely trees. The wind rose higher and higher.

23

A Light in a Dark Window

Blacky sighed with relief when he saw that little Drago had finally fallen asleep. He rose from his chair and stretched, for drowsiness was already beginning to take hold of him. That was why he began to walk up and down the long room.

He had to stay at home because his mother was working on the night shift and he had to take care of his little brother. However, that was not the only reason that kept him home that night. He was lazy and a sleepyhead. He was not as enthusiastic about nocturnal adventures as were his four friends. There was still another reason more significant and important than the rest. It was that blue letter that lay somewhere among the springs of his bed.

The tall, thin boy approached the bed, knelt on one knee, and groped for the envelope among the rusty iron bedsprings. He got it out, stood up, and took it to the table on which stood a kerosene lamp, which cast a pale light over the room. Though he had read the letter twice that morning and several times that afternoon, he read it again with great interest. He did not know why he had hidden it—for there was no one at home except his little brother—but each time he took it back and hid it among the bedsprings.

Blacky sat down, propped his elbows on the table, and began to read, moving his lips all the while.

"Blacky!

"With this letter you will also get a little note. This note is a warning like the one your friends received

144

this morning. Do not tell them that you received this letter, but only show the warning with the skull and crossbones and hide this letter.

"You are older than those dumb squirts, and you realize that they are sticking their noses where they shouldn't. They might get into trouble. Tonight I didn't take anything at the Leibs' on purpose, in order to knock some sense into those little guys. Just the same, they are beginning to be annoying and in the way. You who are older and smarter have to stop playing that dumb game with them.

"Maybe you can guess who is writing this, and maybe you can't. I will not sign myself in case this letter might get into the wrong hands. Besides, I don't know yet whether you will agree to my proposition or whether you will wish to give me away. Here it is: if you want to work with me (and you won't work for nothing), place a light in the window tonight about eleven o'clock. I will know then that you agree, and I will come to talk over all the rest with you. If you don't agree, it might go bad for you. Much worse than with the rest, for now you know more than the rest!

"Hope to see you soon.

"Try to destroy the messages of the other four."

The lean lad stared for a long time at the last lines of the mysterious letter. He had decided at once that he would agree to this proposal, not only because he was afraid of the threat, but also because all this chasing after the thieves seemed to him to be pretty childish and because he believed that he could make some easy money in this way. How many times, while lying in the grass or in bed, he had thought of ways to get hold of some money—but without working! Now suddenly the possibility presented itself. He had only to reach for it.

True, this was what he had thought that morning, but a little while ago, as night was falling, he had felt something like pangs of conscience. It appeared to him that it was not fair to deceive his friends, that it was not honest to leave them in the lurch and, moreover, to work against them. Then he remembered that his friends were really playing, that they were still too young to take all of this seriously. He would not be a traitor, but he was simply too old to play. He already knew what life was about.

He soon succeeded in quieting his misgivings. But it took no little effort to keep from thinking about Cockroach and Bozo, who were huddled somewhere in the bushes and stalking the mad poet.

He did not think for a minute that Mario could be the night prowler and chicken thief, but he did not want to tell the boys anything since he had received the letter that morning. It was all the same whom the little kids suspected.

Blacky examined the handwriting. It was obviously disguised. It was written by a fairly skillful and experienced hand, which had tried to slant the letters in a direction opposite to what was usual. He could not recognize the writing, which was not at all strange, but still he had his suspicions—one person in particular. He believed that was the only possible solution, though he was certain someone else was behind that person. Above all, he was very, very curious. And he was also flattered that this person was turning to him and that the letter emphasized that he was "older" than the rest!

His thoughts were interrupted by the gentle strokes of the little wooden clock. It was eleven. He sprang up abruptly, almost overturning the chair, snatched the kerosene lamp from the table, and took it to the window. Its dim light flickered in the darkness as though it were winking at a shimmering star.

Then Blacky sat on the bed, not thinking about anything any more. Aloud he said, "I don't care!"

Suddenly, a whistle sounded, low, soft, but still quite clear. It sounded again. It came closer and closer. Now it was in front of the house. Then a shadow fell across the window. The face was not clearly visible, but Blacky recognized the nocturnal visitor. He had not been mistaken. The newcomer pushed open the window and jumped into the room.

"Hello, Blacky," he whispered softly as he came forward. The boy stood up, and he tapped him on the shoulder.

"Hello," Blacky answered hoarsely.

"Are you surprised?"

"Well . . . yes and no. I thought it was you."

"And I thought, too, that you'd be smart and listen to me. This playing around with those young fools is not for you."

Blacky did not reply, and the newcomer continued:

"You're much older, smarter. What do you get out of playing cops and robbers? How silly and childish! I'd like to give the little ones a good spanking for it. I thought that those warnings would knock some sense into them. I wrote to them the way they do in the funny papers. I thought it would work. . . . Well, that's that. . . . By the way, did you destroy the messages?"

"I burned them," Blacky replied, looking at the ground.

"Good. I knew that I could count on you. And what have the kids decided to do?"

"They think that Mario is the thief. They were hoping to catch him at it tonight."

"Ha-ha!" The newcomer laughed. "He hangs around Lucy's house practically every night, and he reads poetry. Ha-ha-ha! Did you think that he . . . ha-ha-ha . . ."

"I didn't!"

"You see, you see how dumb they are . . ."

"Listen!" Blacky interrupted him. "You're always saying

how dumb they are, childish and all that, and still you're worried about what they're doing. As if you were afraid of them, huh?"

"Don't be funny!" the young fellow with the mustache shot back unconvincingly, and then hesitated while he was thinking of an answer. "Me afraid of them? Boloney! I just wouldn't want anything to happen to them. After all"—he lowered his voice—"I'm not alone in this."

"I know."

"Is that so? And do you know who's in it with me?"

"No, I don't."

"Well, that's what I'm afraid of, see? He's a tough guy without a heart. Even I'm scared of him. He might hurt them badly. I wanted them to lay off to keep them out of danger. After all, my brother is involved!"

"Who is the man?" Blacky asked resolutely, looking the newcomer in the eye for the first time.

"Well, I can't tell you now. That is," he added, while his eyes flashed in the dim light, "I don't know myself. There's a lot I don't know. I only know that all the loot is kept in an abandoned house by the lake. . . . I shouldn't have told you that. Don't blab, for you can't fool around with him. Here . . ."

Blacky jerked back, for the young man took out of his back pocket a black shiny revolver, which gleamed strangely and unpleasantly in the pale light of the kerosene lamp.

"That . . . why . . . ?" Blacky stuttered, drawing back toward the bed.

"Why so scared? This isn't for you. At least not as long as you do what you're told. . . . Naturally, I carry it just in case, but *he*"—the boy strongly stressed this last word—"he would use it. For instance, he knows now that I am here. He knows that you will probably work with us. And if you should suddenly get it into your head to squeal on us . . ."

The young man did not finish but toyed with the re-

volver. Placing his forefinger on the trigger, he began twirl-
ing it. Blacky stared dumfounded at this dangerous game.
Tiny drops of sweat broke out on his forehead.

"Put it away," he blurted out. "Stop playing around!"

"Don't be scared. It's locked."

"Just the same, put it away."

The newcomer stuck the gun in his pocket and sat on the
table. Then he said seriously, "Come on, let's talk. I have,
that is, we have a job for you, understand?"

"I understand," the tall boy replied meekly, not daring to
sit down. "What's up?"

"We probably won't be working this territory any longer.
There's nothing more to be done here. But we haven't paid
a visit to the Leibs yet. Last night I could have picked up all
kinds of things when that crazy Cockroach left the yard gate
open. The dumbbell wanted to photograph us at night. And
without a flash! Ha-ha-ha! Anyway, it wasn't because I was
soft that I didn't take anything. I looked over the locks on
the stable door. There is a cow and a horse there—we've got
to get them!"

Blacky lowered his eyes.

"We've decided to do it tomorrow. At night, naturally. I
wouldn't want those little fools to get it into their skulls to
poke their noses in there. It would be best if they all went
somewhere together. You could steer them away."

"Me?"

"Naturally, you could do it. You're the oldest, and they'll
listen to you."

"And if they won't go? Don't forget, they'll be pretty discouraged over tonight's failure. Tomorrow they might not
want to try anything."

"Just the same, they'll certainly listen to you. I'm sure
you'll manage. After all, you have to. This is your first job."

"And what'll I get?"

"Wait a minute, wait a minute! You're pretty sharp,

aren't you? You'll get plenty, plenty. Don't worry. Well, O.K.?"

The wooden clock hiccupped twice, and the young man stood up. It was already half-past eleven, and he was obviously in a hurry, so he snapped quickly:

"Well?"

"O.K., I'll try!" Blacky was looking at the legs of the table.

"O.K. Tomorrow evening we'll meet at . . . let's say . . . let's say in the Leibs' vineyard, on the higher side. Be there exactly at . . . at seven o'clock. Then you'll tell me what you've done. And now I have to go. It's time for me to go home. The old man will wake up and there'll be trouble again."

Ivo walked over to the window, took out a cigarette, and lighted it on the flame of the lamp. Then he placed one leg over the window sill and beckoned to his host with a commanding gesture. Blacky came.

"Where is that camera you stole from Mario?"

"I don't know. I think it's at Cockroach's."

"See to it that you get it. That's a valuable little item. It doesn't have to be tomorrow. Whenever you can. We'd pay you well for it. Well, so long."

"So long," the tall boy answered in a hardly audible, hoarse voice. He stood for a long time before the window while his eyes roamed wistfully over the beauties of the night.

24

On the Right Track

Tom was a coward and he knew it. A few days ago he was shaking at the very thought that he might meet up with a runaway enemy soldier with a bayonet in his hand in the woods. He was amazed at the boldness of his friends, unable to believe that he would ever dare do anything similar to Koko Milich's nocturnal adventure. But tonight he did not even think of turning around and going home. Maybe he was so brave because his own brother was involved; maybe he believed that because of this, it was not so dangerous. Maybe. In any case, he waited for a while behind a dilapidated haystack and then trudged across the plowed field in pursuit of his brother. The latter had lighted another cigarette, which made it all the easier to trail him.

Thoughts whirled about Tom's head in utter confusion. He simply could not realize that his brother—whom, it was true, he did not like very much—was mixed up in such a dirty affair. But that was not the only thing that amazed him. He was horrified and overcome with dismay when he observed that Ivo was going straight toward Blacky's house. Almost beside himself, he saw the kerosene lamp waving in the dark window and heard his brother's uneven whistle. These were undoubtedly prearranged signals, a code, as they say. Then Tom recalled what Cockroach had said: "One of us must be a traitor!" Now everything was clear: the traitor was Blacky. It was he who had informed Ivo of their every step from the beginning. And Ivo was probably informing someone else, too. Who was that someone else? That mysterious, tall *second man* whom Koko spied that night?

Ivo came out of Blacky's house and started across a plowed field. Tom found it hard to follow, for his bare feet kept sinking into the soft earth. Ivo, who wore shoes, was making better time over the furrows and putting more and more distance between himself and his pursuer. Tom began to run, afraid of losing sight of the red glow. He felt easier when he saw his brother turn again toward Rocco Road. To the left of the dusty road were vineyards, woods, and orchards, so that it was easier to follow him, for one could stay closer and not lose sight of him.

Ivo continued to move rapidly; he was obviously in a hurry. He flicked away the cigarette butt, and a few moments later his brother kicked some dirt over it, since it had set fire to a few blades of dry grass. On this spot, where Rocco Road abruptly turned toward Lake Road, there was a downgrade. Ivo ran down the slope, then continued northward on the road. Lake Road went along the forest, making a sharp turn at its end and going toward the lake, that is, toward the lonely, bare hill that rose on the northern side.

"Is he going to the lake?" Tom wondered, remembering Bozo's queer experience with old Isaac. "What if Ivo is now going for a swim!" This was an idea that made him both happy and angry. He would have liked to brag about his discovery to impress the boys; and then again, he was dreadfully sorry because it involved his own brother. Even now he knew that he would find it difficult to inform on his brother and turn him over to the police. Who could tell, they might even put him in jail! "First, let's see what happens!" he finally decided, and ran down the slope after his brother, crouching like a hunted animal.

He did not have to wait long. At the crook in the road Ivo did not turn left, toward the lake, but headed along the northern slope of the lonely hill. There was no road here.

They had to trudge along a narrow goat path full of thorns and rocks. Here Ivo looked around for the first time, and everything almost ended in disaster. His brother barely had time to slip behind a big bush. He was so intent that he had overlooked the possibility Ivo might turn around. Ivo listened intently for a while. As everything was completely still, he continued his brisk pace, and Tom was more careful in his pursuit.

Soon their destination came into view. On this side of the hill, on a little ledge, there was a lonely house. Its owners had lost their lives in the war. For a long time some enemy officers had lived here, and it was known that they had killed some men in front of the house. Tom recalled hearing that at night the ghosts of these murdered men came and knocked on the shutters of the abandoned house. Naturally, he did not believe this, but still he was not very happy about remembering it just now.

In the shadow of the hill, complete darkness reigned, since the moon was hiding away somewhere. Black holes yawned across the house, which no longer had any glass in its windows. Some remaining shutters banged against the walls, for the wind was rising. It was all eerie. Tom began to think of his pleasant, warm, safe bed.

What happened after that forced him not to think of fear. He clenched his jaws, which were quivering strangely, probably from the cold wind. Ivo stood before a door of boards that now served as the entrance to the house. He stopped and whistled: three short and two long. Then he waited and tapped lightly on the boards. After a few moments the door opened. Ivo entered without closing it.

Tom did not stop to think, for he knew that then he would get scared and run away.

"That is still my brother, my brother," he kept repeating to himself. "He would never hurt me. Of course not." Tom crouched as low as he could and scurried up to the house.

Carefully he edged toward the door and held it with his hand to keep it from banging in the wind. He was afraid that Ivo might return and shut it if it made too much noise.

It was completely dark in the entrance hall, and distant voices came from the interior of the house. It seemed to Tom that it would not be too dangerous to enter the house. After taking a few steps, he stopped and listened. He was not mistaken. The voices were coming from the cellar. At the head of the stairs there was more light, for a big window gaped on one side. The boy took another step and hit something hard. It was a wooden fence of some sort. He stooped down to see what it was. There was a sight—a whole flock of chickens! Most prominent of all was the red crest of the beautiful big rooster that was Koko's and Mary's favorite. It was as though Tom had expected to find them right there. He was not surprised even when he realized that the huge white shape in front of him was old Isaac's goat. He was certain that Emmie's pig was somewhere in the house. How he would surprise and delight her if he were to drive her black-eared porker straight into her yard the next morning!

But this was no time to be carried away by such ideas. He had to find out as much as possible. He had to discover who the second man was, for he secretly suspected that this man was more important than his brother. He could not believe that his brother was doing this of his own free will. He secretly hoped that in the end it would be proven that Ivo had been forced to work for the unknown scoundrel.

"I'll go down. Maybe I'll be able to see them from the staircase." He was barefoot and stepped noiselessly. He descended the stairs and stopped at the lower landing. There were only eight more steps to the cellar. He went down them and stood before a door, of which only the lower half remained standing. In the first room, where there were several old barrels, there was nobody. But from the second room there came the weak and flickering light of a candle or a kerosene lamp.

Tom did not dare go further. He felt the cold concrete floor under his soles, and his jaws kept quivering, this time probably because of the cold floor. He did not want to enter because one of the two might come out at any moment, so he pressed against the wall and, edging his head toward the opening, carefully watched the entrance into that other room.

He could hear creaking, rumbling, and grunting. They were moving or carrying something. Then the noise ceased, and in the complete silence he could hear two men panting heavily. Finally Ivo's voice came.

"Did you get a good price for the goat?"

"Yes," a thicker, deeper voice replied.

Tom trembled. At last, he heard *him*.

"How much?"

"I don't know yet, but it will be plenty. And did you take care of the little squirts?"

Tom had to clench his jaws to keep his teeth from chattering loudly against each other. The voice of the mystery man gave him goose-pimples.

"It's all set. Blacky has agreed. Tomorrow he will talk them into going somewhere together. He'll report to me whether he has succeeded or not."

"When?"

"Before dark."

"Fine. I got a new hacksaw. I think that we'll be able to get the locks off in ten minutes. Only don't forget to bring some hay here. Maybe the horse will have to stay for several days. It'll be more dangerous to sell than the cow."

"I told Blacky about the camera, too. He'll try to get hold of it. We could sell it for good money, couldn't we?"

"Sure. It's the easiest thing to get rid of. You take it to

town, in your pocket, and sell it. Besides, we're not even the ones who stole it, ha-ha-ha. . . ."

Tom grew stiff on hearing this laugh. The muffled voice of the mystery man made him suspect someone, but it seemed too fantastic to him. However, the laughter shook him. Something began to buzz in his head. He could barely follow the conversation in the nearby room any more. Luckily, he did hear Ivo say:

"Shall we go?"

Instead of an answer, the light shone brighter. It had been moved closer to the exit. In no more than the twinkling of an eye Tom was out of the house and on his way.

"No, I can't. I can't," he kept repeating to himself while he ran. He felt something choking him. He wanted to cry. He knew only one thing: he must not tell anyone what he had discovered that night. That secret must remain forever in his broken heart.

25

When Fools Give Counsel

The boys—especially Cockroach and Bozo—were completely discouraged by the curious events of the night before. Having become convinced in such a peculiar way that the poet Mario was innocent, they did not even dare think of another venture. Everything seemed pointless now. There was nothing to do but to wait until the police were able to come to their aid. And so the boys fell into that limp, helpless indecision to which their parents had surrendered long ago, exhausted by the ravages of the recent war.

Nevertheless, they still faced one more night filled with adventure and excitement—only none of them knew it as yet.

When Blacky arrived at Bozo's in the afternoon, he found him sitting on the doorstep, holding his head between his hands and staring dully at a horned cricket, which was lying on its back in the dust and vainly trying to turn over onto its legs.

"Greetings," said the tall newcomer, spitting right next to the sprawling cricket. "How are you, fellow?"

His voice had a special quality, a certain forced gaiety, but the lad with the glasses did not raise his head. He only replied with a mumbled, "M-m-m."

Blacky knew the reason for the boy's bad mood, but anyway he asked casually:

"No go?"

"No go."

"What happened? What did you find out?"

"It isn't Mario." Bozo sighed and added sadly, "Are we dopes!"

The tall boy realized that his time had come. He had to give new life to an interest grown weak and cold. He spat once more, coughed slightly, sat on the doorstep, and threw one leg over the other. Then he spoke softly.

"Look, fellow, don't be sad. I've thought of something."

Bozo was not as surprised by what his older friend said as by the tone in which he said it. Blacky was always reserved, rather arrogant and conceited, and he always addressed his friends in a cold, hard tone of voice. Now, suddenly, his voice was warm and friendly. He topped everything by putting his long, thin arm around Bozo's frail shoulders. He said in a pleasant voice:

"Come on, come on; everything will be all right. I think we'll find out everything tonight. You know that until now I haven't really taken part in all this. I didn't trust in your wild guesses. But now it's different. I think I know something for sure about those hoodlums, the robbers, and so . . ."

"Who are they?" Bozo asked feverishly, lifting his head. Behind the thick glasses his eyes burned with curiosity.

"Wait a minute! After all, I wouldn't want to be wrong. I am sure, but still, you know how it is. . . . You fell for something twice."

"Come on and tell." Bozo grew excited again, stood up, turned the powerless cricket over on its legs, and sat down. "Please, tell just me."

"I'll tell you all or no one. Anyway, it isn't long till nighttime. You'll all know everything before midnight."

"And where will we go this evening?"

"First of all, we all have to go together tonight. So it would be best if you brought the other boys here for a meeting."

"When?"

"Right away. The sooner the better. It will soon be six
o'clock. There's not much time before dark."

Bozo jumped quickly to his feet. He was ready to run off
immediately and do as he had been told. He was proud that
aloof, haughty Blacky had turned to him first.

"Wait," said the tall boy, also getting up. "All three of
them have to come for sure. I'll call Koko myself, and you
go after Cockroach and Tom. And come as soon as possible."

Bozo was about to leave when Blacky stopped him again
with a strange question.

"Do you have a strong, long rope somewhere at home?"

"No, I don't think we have." Bozo was dumfounded.

"Then tell Cockroach to bring one with him. He doesn't
have to bring it here, but tell him to get it ready for tonight.
Now go on, hurry."

Bozo ran down to the road and scurried off in search of
his friends, while Blacky went to the fence, leaned his elbows on it, and with two fingers began to pick the ripe seeds
from a sunflower, placing them between his teeth and
crunching them. He was not any too calm and collected.

It was not easy for Bozo to talk Cockroach into leaving
the armchair in which he was settled. After last night's
stupid adventure, he had decided never again to engage in
such kid stuff. It was more exciting to read about real
American gangsters than to sit under a pear tree and watch
a widow sling flowerpots at a crazy poet.

However, his resolution was shaken by the fact that it was
Blacky who was giving orders this time. Secretly he yearned
for Blacky's friendship and could not pass up this chance.
Besides, he had been asked to get the rope, and this made
him more eager than anything else. The fact that they
would need a rope showed how serious things were.

"We'll be climbing up something," he whispered to Bozo,
after having agreed to this new proposal.

"Or else climbing down!" Bozo rejoined.

At Tom's, an unpleasant surprise awaited them. He was lying in bed sick and could not join them. He replied to all their urging by saying that he was very ill, that his stomach and head hurt, and that he could not get up.

"You're just spoiled," Cockroach declared knowingly, and waved his hand.

Bozo was wiser and decided not to press him too hard, so he concluded gravely:

"What can we do? If he's sick, he's sick. We'll have to do without him."

"And where are you going?" the boy in the bed asked in a weak voice.

"We don't know yet," Bozo replied.

"What do you care!" Cockroach said bitterly. "Let's go!"

A pair of sad eyes gazed after them for a long while; they seemed sick with sorrow.

Cockroach stopped by his house to get his bicycle. He placed his smaller friend on the handle bars, and soon they were gliding down the road. In the twinkling of an eye they were in the yard with the sunflowers. Blacky and Koko were sitting next to one another in friendly conversation. The tall boy was rather impatient. When he spied the bicycle, he jumped to his feet and ran toward the newcomers.

"Where's Tom?" he asked immediately.

"Sick," both replied at the same time.

When Blacky learned that Tom was really in bed and that he could not get up, he calmed down a bit and invited his friends to sit down. Then he told them briefly what was up. At ten o'clock they would all meet at the crossing of Green Hill Road and the wagon road that led to the next village. The foundations of an unfinished pillbox were situated there, and Blacky fixed that as their meeting place. Exactly at ten. Cockroach was to bring the rope.

"And what do we need a rope for?" Koko asked, while his left hand scratched behind his right ear.

"Maybe we'll have to tie someone up," Blacky said mysteriously, and stood up. It was apparent that they were not going to get anything else out of him. "Now I still have to go somewhere. Well, at ten o'clock then. Be on time."

26

Even the Grapevines Have Ears

It is neither nice nor honest to eat grapes in someone else's vineyard. It is especially bad when a girl does it. Even if she eats only one bunch or just picks off a grape here and there, this does not lessen the shame.

But Emmie did not think about that. Of course, if she had thought about it, she would not have done it. The entire misfortune lay in her not thinking. It was no sin to want to eat grapes, and she knew that neither her mother nor her aunt could afford to buy any. The nearest grapes to be had were in the Leibs' big vineyard, and Emmie headed straight for it. She had to cross over two fences, taking care not to tear her rose-colored dress in the meantime, and, above all, she had to make certain that no one observed this shameful visit.

Emmie knew very well that she would certainly get grapes from Cockroach if she only asked. And his parents would most certainly permit her to go into the vineyard and eat her fill. However, she was too proud to ask, for she would be showing that her mother was too poor to buy her a bit of fruit.

It was easy enough to cross the first fence, since the boards were fairly low in several spots. After running through the orchard, Emmie came upon the second fence. This one was much higher, and it took some time before she found a slit in the fence big enough for her to gain a foothold and climb over the high boards. She was surprised at her own skill. Swaying on top of the fence, she got up her nerve and jumped, landing on her feet.

"Just like those thieves in the night!" she said to herself, and she smiled, but immediately she remembered her pig and grew sad. This was no time to think about it. All about her there hung clusters of grapes.

Here and there she plucked a grape. She did not want to pick a whole bunch until she found the most beautiful and the largest in the entire vineyard. But it was not so easy to pick out. Emmie soon found herself at the upper end of the vineyard, where the grapevines grew in the shadow of the tall pines and where nothing was ripe yet. She frowned and was about to go back when she heard footsteps. Someone was coming.

Someone was coming down the road and would certainly see her if she tried to run. She did not stop to think. Quickly she crouched down in the shadow of the pines and pressed against a slender tar-covered trunk. Instantly she remembered her rose-colored dress, and so she sat in the grass.

It was Blacky, a boy whom she had never especially cared for. Now, moreover, she was angry at him. Here the grapes were, within reach, and yet she could not eat a single one because of that big lug! Worst of all, apparently he had no intention of going on. On the contrary, it seemed to her as though he too had come a-stealing; but it was not so. He stood in front of the vineyard, on the road, and looked around. All of a sudden he lifted his arm and began to wave. He saw someone.

Soon Ivo came down the road. Emmie was a bit angry at him also because he was not wearing the cap she had so generously presented to him.

"You're here!" Ivo exclaimed.

"Naturally," Blacky replied, spitting in the dust.

The girl could hear every word. As the conversation unfolded, her brown eyes widened more and more.

"Fixed everything?" Ivo inquired further, raising his voice and smiling slyly.

"It's all fixed. The boys will be at the crossing at ten o'clock. Everybody, except your brother. He's . . ."

"Yes, I know, he's sick. Ate too much fruit. What did you decide to do?"

"I'll tell them that I suspect the milkmen from the next village who come here every day. Of course, they'll be disappointed. But they're used to it by now. I told them to bring along a rope, as though we were going to tie the thieves up."

"Ha-ha-ha, that's good. You'll get something from tonight's take. Both the cow and the horse can be sold for good money."

"But," Blacky suddenly said more quietly, "it seems to me that all this wasn't necessary."

"What wasn't necessary?" the other boy demanded, furrowing his eyebrows.

"I mean, there was no need to fool them. They wouldn't have tried anything anyway."

"Maybe you're sorry?" said Ivo, laughing contemptuously.

Blacky said nothing for a while, and then he spoke up.

"Well. That's that. Only promise me that this is your last job around here."

"Naturally"—Ivo smiled with satisfaction—"naturally. The last and the biggest. Now there isn't any more to take. Only don't forget the camera. That little thing is worth a good deal."

Blacky made no reply but nodded his head dumbly. His shoulders were drooping slightly, and he seemed to be smaller and shorter than he really was.

"Tomorrow I'll come to you. We'll tell each other about our adventures of the evening." Ivo patted his reluctant friend on the shoulder. "They ought to be good! And now, let's go. We have to get ready. Ha-ha-ha. . . ." He suddenly laughed again. "What a good idea . . . I mean that about the rope. . . . Ha-ha-ha . . ."

And he hurried down the road. Blacky stood for a while longer, not lifting his head. Then he spat far and set off slowly in the other direction. From time to time he stopped and shook his head, as though nodding in agreement with someone.

And from the shadows of the tall pines two big brown eyes were watching. For a moment Emmie could not realize that all of this was true, that all of this had happened before her very eyes. Dimly, however, she sensed that in some way she was partly to blame. She did not quite know why, but she felt it. She also felt the need to do something about it, to make things right again. Soon after, she was running through the grapevines, paying no attention to the enticing smell of the ripe grapes.

27

A Victory over Self

The head on the big white pillow swarmed with all kinds of thoughts. Most were unpleasant and sad. Tom Bran knew that it was not honest to keep his discovery of the night before a secret and to withhold from his friends the names of the thieves who had done so much harm in the whole region. He knew that he, too, was now a traitor and that he was no different at all from Blacky. He blushed whenever he remembered that Cockroach, Koko, and Bozo certainly would not have acted like that. He was ashamed and angry at himself, but still he could not make up his mind to do anything. He could not hand over his brother. He imagined as he looked through the window how they would take Ivo away bound in handcuffs and prod him with rifle butts. And as he imagined this terrible scene, the tears welled up in his eyes. Besides, if it were true . . . if that other voice he heard last night. . . . No, no, he did not dare even think of it! It was too much to bear.

Tom rolled over in bed and buried his head in the fresh-smelling sheets. At that moment he wished he were dead, that something terrible would happen. If the ceiling would fall and bury him! That was all he was good for. Of course, he was not sick, and his stomach did not hurt him at all. How he wished that he were really sick! But, in vain. He was sorry that his mother had not yet returned from town. She said that she would sleep at his aunt's no more than two nights. Wouldn't one night have been enough? He was angry at her. She ought to know, she ought to sense that he was in trouble.

Suddenly, just as the unhappy boy had rolled over in bed once again and was staring at the ceiling, hoping against hope that it would crash down over him, he heard something strike the window. After a short pause, there was another tap, and then . . . no doubt about it, someone was throwing pebbles.

In a trice Tom was out of bed. Outside it was already quite dark so that he could not tell whether there was someone in the yard or not. When his eyes grew a bit accustomed to the dark, he could see the figure of a girl. Emmie was beckoning to him with quick motions to come down as soon as possible.

As he flew down the stairs and passed through the kitchen, he almost ran into his father, who looked at him in wonder.

"Aren't you supposed to be sick? Or maybe you have already grown well, doctor? Maybe you have healed yourself?" he concluded mockingly.

"I feel better," Tom replied in some confusion. Judging by the fact that his father had returned from the barbershop, it must be eight o'clock already. "But I'm going to bed again. I'm only going outside for a bit."

His father looked at him quizzically once more and shook his head.

"You might at least dress yourself," he said, but the lad did not hear. He had already sped away into the yard.

Now it was his turn to be amazed as he beheld Emmie. She was out of breath and scratched about the arms. Her rose-colored dress was torn in one spot, so that a strip hung to her knees. She could hardly wait for Tom to reach her.

When he approached, she placed a finger on his lips and drew him toward the garden gate. He looked around involuntarily. Her behavior was strange and mysterious.

"Pss-s-st!" said Emmie, seeing that he was about to speak. "Pss-s-st!"

Once within the garden, she took her finger from his lips and heaved a deep sigh of relief.

"I know who the robbers are," she said so firmly and convincingly that Tom drew back a step. How did she know?

"Who?" he asked innocently.

"Ivo and Blacky. Ivo is the ringleader, and Blacky is helping him. He is a spy. In war they shoot such people."

Tom was flabbergasted. This was too much. Now he was not the only one to know the truth. Emmie, too, knew a good deal. Meanwhile, she went on talking.

"Tonight they are going to steal the Leibs' cow and horse, and Blacky has talked the boys into going into the next village this evening. He's pretending that the milkmen are the thieves they are looking for. He's going to meet the boys at the pillbox at ten o'clock. You must stop them!"

"I'm sick. I don't feel well," the boy replied warily, and lowered his eyes.

"It seems to me that you aren't sick at all. You're bluffing," Emmie blurted out suddenly, looking straight at him.

"I . . ." He wanted to think of something.

"You're not to blame for having blabbed everything to me. I'm to blame," she continued quite firmly, as though she felt no shame over this at all, "for telling Ivo. No, don't be so surprised: I told him everything. I wanted . . . I don't know myself what I wanted. I was dumb. I think that Blacky wasn't working for Ivo then. At least I think so."

"How do you know all this?" Tom finally asked.

"Never mind. I eavesdropped. It's not important. But. . . . Are you going to sleep?"

"I feel a little sick again. It will go away by morning," Tom quickly answered. "Good night." These last words barely crossed his lips.

He dressed and threw himself on the bed, placing the

alarm clock beside him. It was ten minutes past eight. He
had nearly two more hours to wait. His plan was already
completely formed in his head. Emmie had won out. It did
not even occur to him that he might fall asleep tonight. It
was different from several days ago. Tonight there was serious business ahead.

The time passed unbelievably slowly.

28

On the Usefulness of a Rope

"Here he is, he's coming!" Bozo shouted. Oddly enough, it seemed as though he saw better at night than during the day. Or maybe it was just his hearing.

Cockroach, who had grown impatient, lifted his head and peered into the darkness. Koko was thinking about something else: if nothing came of this night's venture either, things would not go well with him. At that moment, without any doubt, his father had the thick strap all ready for him, so this particular night had a double meaning for Koko. If they caught the thieves, he would be spared a licking. And it would be the licking of his life, of this he had not the slightest doubt. His father had specifically forbidden him to leave the house at night.

"Nuts," Cockroach abruptly exclaimed. "It's only Tom."

"By golly, it is!" Bozo chimed in.

"But isn't he sick?" Koko asked. Nobody had expected Tom. They were waiting for Blacky, who was already a good ten minutes late. No one replied to this last question, for the supposedly sick boy was quite close to the fallen telegraph pole on which the three boys were sitting motionless, like crows. Behind them were the foundations of the unfinished pillbox.

"Hello, fellows," said Tom with apparent calm, carefully looking at each of the three in turn. "Blacky not here yet?"

"See for yourself!" said Cockroach sullenly, for he was still angry at Tom.

"Did you get well?" asked Bozo, but one could feel in his voice that it was all the same to him whether Tom had gotten well or not.

"Fellows . . ." Tom began in a still voice. "Fellows . . . I have something to tell you."

"A new discovery?" Koko grumbled, thinking of the wide brown strap.

"No kidding, listen to me," Tom continued, sitting down on the pole and looking in the direction from which he had come. "This is serious. I know who the robber is. I am sure about one; as for the other . . ."

"You don't say!" Cockroach exclaimed sarcastically, and slapped his knee. "And who's the one you're sure about?"

"Ivo," the lad said hoarsely.

Silence reigned. Only the crickets could be heard.

"Your brother?" Bozo summoned the strength to ask.

"Yes. And Blacky is in with him."

"Then he's the other one?" Cockroach laughed, for all of this seemed silly to him again. "Is that it?"

"No, it's not like that." Tom leaped to his feet. "Blacky is only a stooge; he's a spy. That's how they know every move we make, every plan."

Again for several moments only the crickets could be heard.

"How do you know?" Koko asked suddenly, lazily scratching himself behind the ear. "Huh?"

"I found out last night. I followed Ivo. . . . He had a meeting with Blacky. Then he went to that deserted house beyond the lake. That's where the chickens are, and Isaac's goat, and your rooster . . ." He turned toward Koko, hoping fervently that they would at last believe him. "Tonight they are going to try to steal your cow and horse, Cockroach. I heard Ivo talking to the other one . . ."

"Why are you telling us all this now?" Cockroach asked, still suspicious.

Tom hesitated a bit and then he said sorrowfully:

"He's still my brother . . ."

These words hit the three boys hard. Each of them felt sympathy and admiration for their good friend. But there was no time to ponder on his virtues, for rapid footsteps could be heard down the road.

"Blacky!" Koko exclaimed.

Those were very exciting moments, moments that demanded presence of mind, determination, and boldness. The first to gather his wits about him was Bozo, who took a few steps forward in the direction of the newcomer. Not getting up, Koko carefully watched to see what would happen. Tom drew back a step, feeling his courage slip away from him.

"Well," said Blacky, turning straight to him. "Look who's here! Are you all right again?"

While Blacky was watching Tom and Tom was watching Blacky, and Bozo and Koko were watching both of them, nobody took notice of Cockroach, who was leaning over on the other side of the fallen pole, doing something on the ground.

"I'm not completely well yet," Tom finally said, "but I didn't want to miss this."

Blacky did not perceive the mocking expression on Tom's face, for everything was quite dark. There was no moon.

"Fellows," Blacky declared in a solemn voice, "the time has come to tell you of my plan. Actually, it's very simple. I don't want to tell you yet whom I suspect, but I can tell you that the thieves are not from here. True, they know us well, for every day . . ."

"The milkmen?" Tom suddenly inquired, having rid himself of his previous fear.

"Hm, you're pretty sharp. Well, anyway, let's not talk about it until we catch them at it. I expect them to be coming along this road, so I suggest that we go down a bit, to that ditch. . . . Oh, yes, by the way, did you bring the rope, Cockroach?"

"Yes, I did." Cockroach, whose back had been turned to the other four, now spoke for the first time.

"Here, let me have it. Can we tie up two with it?"

What happened then came so swiftly and unexpectedly that the dumfounded onlookers were rooted to the spot, dumb and motionless, even after it was all over. Cockroach slowly rose, turned lazily, and went toward Blacky, carrying the rope in front of him over his outstretched hands. It seemed as though he were carrying a precious, breakable object or a slumbering baby. Blacky held out his hands to take hold of the rope, and at that very moment Cockroach skillfully and quickly slipped it over the tall boy's head and quickly tightened it. Clearly it was a noose he had been making just a few moments ago. Before he knew what had happened, Blacky was lying on the ground, for Cockroach had tripped him.

"Over here!" the victor called to his stupefied friends. "Help me!"

All of them fell on Blacky, who had begun to thrash about. He was not able to cry out or to swear, for they stuffed his mouth with a handkerchief. In the twinkling of an eye they bound him in the long rope, so that, motionless and wrapped from head to toe, he looked like an Egyptian mummy. Only two eyes flashed above the handkerchief. What could be seen in them was not fury alone. There was also desperation and sadness and maybe regret.

"There!" said Cockroach, straightening himself up and wiping the palms of his hands.

"What will we do with him?" asked Koko, who was unusually glad about all this and who had completely forgotten about his home and the wide brown strap.

"We'll put him in this pillbox for now and come back for him later. It's better to keep him here. Otherwise, he might spoil everything. Come on, take hold of him."

At this last suggestion of Cockroach's, the boys readily picked up and carried the long bundle into the unfinished pillbox beside the road.

"Let's hope there won't be any rain!" Bozo remarked, inspecting the sky.

"Even if there is, it won't hurt him any. It will wash him, and then maybe his conscience will be a bit cleaner," Koko joked. One could feel that they were all rather pleased that they could take revenge on Blacky—not only for his betrayal, but also because they had been in awe of him for so long and had always given in to him. However, they could not afford to lose time. They had yet to catch the real thieves.

"Let's go!" Tom exclaimed hotly, and almost flew down the road. The other lads hurried after him, and no one gave the trussed-up traitor another look. Everywhere one could hear only the crickets—the crickets and the quick short footsteps of four boys who were off to face new adventures.

When Cockroach caught up with Tom, he placed a hand on his shoulder and said softly:

"If you made all this up, I'll cut both your ears off."

29

A Mad Chase

The entire countryside seemed peaceful and still. Only the stars looked down upon what was happening at Green Hill.

The boys hurried as fast as they could. They did not know exactly when the robbers intended to break into Cockroach's yard, so they had to get there as soon as possible.

"We could have asked Blacky," Bozo remembered. "He must know. We could have made him tell."

"He doesn't know," Tom snapped curtly and firmly.

"We'd better run," Koko suggested.

To be safe, they did not go directly along Green Hill Road, but they raced across the plowland, so that they might go around Cockroach's house and enter the yard from the other side. Thus there was no danger of their coming upon the thieves ahead of time.

When they passed in front of the house, they crossed the road and began to creep around the back. They jumped over the orchard fence and headed for the wall around the yard. As he was best acquainted with his own house, Cockroach assumed the role of leader. He knew of a place on this side where it was possible to climb over the wall into the yard, but he felt that was superfluous.

"Let Koko climb up that apple tree. From there he can see into the yard. When they appear, he can wave his hand. We'll rush to the gate and shut them in the yard!"

"A trap!" Tom rejoiced, but immediately grew sad. He

recalled the vision of his brother being led away to prison in chains.

It was not entirely clear why Cockroach assigned Koko the role of scout, but no one paid any attention. After all, someone had to do the job, and Cockroach was now in command. Everyone agreed with the proposal, and Koko began to scramble up the tree. It was a twisted, gnarled apple tree, and he reached its top branches in a jiffy.

The remaining three, who were watching his ascent, were not at all surprised when, having settled himself, he began to wave his hand excitedly. Each felt his heart pound harder. Cockroach pulled himself together and asked as quietly as he could:

"You see them?"

"No," came the reply from out of the leaves, "but the gate is open."

"Get down!" Cockroach commanded, and impatiently watched Koko as he climbed down much more slowly than he had ascended.

Apparently they had arrived precisely while the thieves were at work. To be sure, they could not see the stable from here. But probably they, Ivo and the other one, were inside this very minute. They must run around the wall as quickly as possible, have a look into the yard from the open gate, and catch them like mice in a trap.

The threesome again sped off with their leader. The wall was a long one; it seemed endless. Finally—the corner. The gate was just a few paces away, then just one more step. Cockroach cautiously took a peek.

He swore and struck the wall with his left fist. He had cause for this: the stable door was wide open, and in the dust of the yard could be seen the tracks of hoofs. They were too late!

One after the other, the boys hung their heads. What Tom had told them was true. They had lost the opportunity

to catch the real thieves. And was not this perhaps their last chance?

Suddenly Tom slapped his forehead and exclaimed:

"The deserted house!"

At first, of course, no one could understand a thing. All Tom had related half an hour ago about his experiences of the night before had been so jumbled and confused that no one had quite taken in what it was all about. He repeated briefly what he had already told them.

Bozo was the first to understand, and he shouted:

"Quick. Let's go!"

"O.K.!" Cockroach caught on and was the first to start running.

"Take Rocco Road!" Tom had time to shout, and the mad chase began all over again.

Quickly they ran across the orchard, dodging the tree trunks like skiers in a slalom. At a spot where the boards were shorter, Cockroach leaped over the fence and found

himself in the vineyard. The other three followed suit. No one noticed a little piece of rose-colored cloth dangling in the fence.

It was harder to run through the vineyard because the rows of vines were much closer together than were the tree trunks. Nevertheless, the boys soon emerged by the pine trees and took to the road. There was no fear that they would encounter anyone, so they began to run along Rocco Road. Bozo and Tom already had a sharp pain in their right sides, under the ribs, but both tried not to lag behind the first two.

Here, on the northern side, the starry, moonless night was even calmer and more tranquil than down by the crossroads at the unfinished pillbox. Not even a cricket could be heard. At first only the pounding of eight feet disturbed the still of the night, and then even that monotonous sound somehow merged into the silence.

It was cool, but sweat ran down the boys' foreheads. Cock-

roach also felt sharp jabs underneath his ribs, but he
clenched his teeth. There was no time to pay any attention
to such trifles now. They passed by Blacky's house. They
could hear little Drago crying inside. Not even this could
claim their attention now. Before them was a great and
noble aim.

Just beyond a short incline there came a sharp slope, and
the path descended to the left toward Lake Road. But the
boys cut across, over the plowed field, where Tom had also
descended the night before. Their bare feet sank deep into
the soft earth, and so they could not run very fast. Besides,
they kept looking more at their feet than in front of them.
Nevertheless, Bozo, whose eyesight by day was poorer than
that of the rest, looked from time to time into the distance,
secure in the knowledge that he could see better at night.

"Stop!" he said, and stood still.

The boys stopped and crouched down, as their friend's
voice was full of apprehension and warning.

"What is it?" all three asked practically at once, while
staring at Bozo.

"Look!" he said by way of reply, and pointed toward the
road.

At the bend of Lake Road, not far from the edge of the
forest, they could see figures moving about. At first two big,
long shapes—a cow and a horse, and then two men.

The pursuers were paralyzed. No one quite knew what
ought to be done now. Cockroach wanted to say how much
better it would have been if Tom had told them everything
earlier: they could have so easily called the militia. But he
said nothing, for he remembered that Tom's brother was
involved and that Tom must have a lot to bear because of
this. It seemed best to him to hurry after them and to find
out who the robbers were. They could report everything
later. But what would they do once they saw them?

The others' thoughts were the same as Cockroach's. No

one was surprised or protested when he proposed that they continue the chase.

"Let's go!" Bozo exclaimed, and the others stood up.

The chase continued down the slope.

It seemed to all of them that their only job was to catch up with the marauders and to have a look at their faces. Caution, which for several days had marked all their actions, now left them entirely. They did not even consider that something dangerous might happen.

Their bare feet sank softly in the furrows, so that their steps could hardly be heard. But once they came out on the road, there was a sound like the falling of distant rain. When they passed the first bend, they caught sight of the two men and their valuable four-legged booty about a hundred yards in front of them. About the same time the robbers spied their pursuers!

It was hard to tell what the thieves had in mind just then. Perhaps they did not quite understand who was on their trail. Perhaps they thought the boys were only the advance guard of another, more dangerous pursuer. In any case, the determination of the pursuers certainly confused them. Dismayed by this turn of events, the two men lost their presence of mind, abandoned the horse and cow, and started running toward the forest and the lake. Perhaps they wanted to cover their tracks and to prevent the boys from discovering their secret hiding place.

"After them! Everybody after them!" Bozo shouted on noticing Cockroach hesitate. The green-eyed boy was looking at his animals, calmly proceeding down the road.

The four set out across the field, then broke into a run toward the forest. When they reached the edge of it, they stopped for a moment, and then they heard the sound of running feet in the distance. The mad chase continued.

When they came to a clearing, they spied the men they were pursuing on the other side. At that moment the shorter of the two—it was Ivo—stopped and turned around. A shot cracked through the air and echoed through the slumbering forest. The boys did not stop but kept on running as fast as they could.

"In the air!" Koko gasped. "They don't dare shoot at us."

This observation gave even more courage to the already bold pursuers. "Yes," Bozo thought, irritated because the sweat was beclouding his glasses. "They say that as long as you can hear it, the bullet's far away. If it's close, you can't hear a thing."

When they reached the thick part of the forest, they heard a rustling and a crackling accompanied by oaths. Something had landed heavily in the fallen leaves. Cockroach was the first to catch up with Ivo. He was stretched prone, his legs wide, while his gun had slid out of his hand and was now lying among some mushrooms several yards from his outstretched hand. Cockroach did not hesitate but immediately threw himself on Ivo and sat on his chest.

"You nut!" Ivo moaned. "Get off. I've wrenched my leg."

Koko and Bozo ran up and stopped beside the now powerless young man. No one even noticed that Tom hardly glanced at his brother but dashed deeper into the forest. Tom ran, though he struggled against the pain under his ribs and the dryness in his throat and mouth. His head swam, while his knees were gradually beginning to give way. He tried not to think. He did not even pay attention to his friends, nor did he care about his brother. He wanted to find out whether his terrible suspicion about the other man was true. He hoped with all his heart to be mistaken. That was why he hurried so, in order to find out the truth. In this moment, perhaps, he was glad that his friends had remained behind. It would be easier for him to find out by himself.

The forest grew more sparse, and there came into view the silvery surface of the tranquil lake, in which the stars were reflected.

About ten paces from the panting pursuer, a thickset man, also worn out by this mad chase, leaned on a cane. He probably had been using the cane to drive the cow. He started when he heard footsteps and slowly looked about. The meager light revealed a long mustache and dark hair.

"Father!" Tom cried desperately, and rushed toward the tall man with outstretched arms.

Blacky lay with his eyes open wide and observed the night life around him. His head teemed with all kinds of thoughts, which he could not shake off. He had wavered before, aware that he was doing his friends a bad turn, but now his conscience began to gnaw at him like a biting frost.

"And what will Ivo say?" This thought flashed through his brain again and again. Whenever he recalled his meeting with that youth, who had finally become a friend, who had even sought his help, Blacky would forget about his conscience and his friends and desire to free himself. "Something has to be done. I must let them know, I must warn them. Oh, what will Ivo and his mysterious partner think of me when they learn how clumsy I am and that they couldn't count on me?"

He was seized with fury against himself and began to beat his head in a frenzy against the well-trodden ground. That is how his eyes suddenly fell upon a bayonet, which protruded from a big empty oil drum. In the twinkling of an eye it was clear to him that he could free himself. "Maybe I'll get there yet," he thought, "maybe I'll get there yet." He recalled Ivo's mentioning the abandoned house on the other side of the lake. They probably took their loot there. He did not doubt that he could run faster than the other boys; he could arrive there before the pursuers. True, Ivo had forbidden him to go there, but this was a special case. In all probability the mysterious partner would even praise him.

Everything was even simpler than it had seemed to him a few minutes before. Rolling across the ground, he knocked over the drum and the bayonet fell out. He managed to lay his tethered legs alongside the blade. With a little pressure the tight bonds were cut. He was soon free. As he ran, he took the handkerchief out of his mouth and breathed deeply. "I'll get there, I'll get there yet." He encouraged himself, trying to guess how long he had lain in the pillbox.

As it was, luck served him well. At the crossroads in front of Emmie's house stood a truck loaded with wood. The truck driver had just made some repair, and the motor was already humming. Blacky ran up, stepped on the running board, and asked the driver where he was going and whether he would take him along.

"Climb up!" the man behind the wheel replied, having just pointed in the direction of Lake Road, exactly where Blacky was headed. Blacky sat on the fender while hanging on to the edge of the open window.

"Tell me when you want to get off," the driver called in a casual but friendly tone. The truck started, the puddles splashed beneath its wheels, and the wind whistled. In no time at all they were on the big bend not far from the edge of the forest. The motor coughed, and the truck took the curve carefully and slowly; Blacky jumped off saying nothing, not even thanks.

He ran into the dark forest a little below the spot where the hunters and the hunted had entered. He hoped that by going along the lake he would reach the abandoned house before them. He ran recklessly, paying no heed to the gnarled fingers of the roots, which kept grasping at his ankles. Before him flashed the mirrored surface of the lake. Suddenly he stopped and lifted his head; he heard voices and blows clearly. Some fifty yards in front of him a man was beating a boy with a stick.

"Wretch!" Mirko Bran shouted hoarsely, and struck

powerfully at the boy who stood before him. "Take that! And that!"

The blows fell on Tom's outstretched arms and on his head. He felt a dull pain penetrate his forehead; then the starry sky and the lake danced before his eyes and became a jumbled mass; finally everything sank into a colorless darkness.

Thus Tom did not see a second strange figure that leaped on the man with the mustache. It was a huge dog that seemed to spring right out of the ground.

A second after Hobo's attack Blacky arrived. He recognized the man who had been beating Tom. Even though it was not quite clear to him how and why all this was happening, he was sure about one thing: he had to help Tom and save him from the enraged barber. These new feelings welled up inside him faster than he was able to understand the actual events. In this way he might redeem himself with his comrades and make up for his mean betrayal. Perhaps this was his only, his last chance to make amends for what he had done, his last chance to come clean with his friends. In one moment he was again completely on their side.

Tom did not see how Blacky came to the aid of the dog, and how the lad and the animal pinned the mustachioed thief to the ground. He did not hear the gentle, trembling voice of old Isaac, who unexpectedly spoke from somewhere in the darkness:

"Poor, poor boy."

And then he added:

"At last you've gotten what you deserved, Mirko."

30

Like All Endings

The sun was already high in the sky and clear daylight filled the room where a boy was lying on a bed. Only his eyes, his nose, and mouth were visible: all the rest of him was swathed in white bandages, which merged with the color of the clean bed sheets. His eyelids lay quietly over closed eyes.

Though undisturbed silence reigned in the room, still the room was not empty. There were more people in it than ever before. Right next to the bed sat an unknown man with a rosy nose and graying hair. Judging by the way he held the hand of the slumbering lad in his own hairy fist and judging by the look on his face, one could conclude that this was the doctor. Over him stood the boy's mother, and her red eyes betrayed that she had been weeping. Not far away sat old Isaac, holding his chin in both hands and trying not to sigh. Against the balcony door leaned the long-haired poet, about whose neck hung a camera. Beside him stood Cockroach and Emmie, while Koko and Bozo were near the stove.

"He is no longer in a coma," the doctor announced with satisfaction. Everyone in the room quickly raised his head. "This is now normal sleep."

"And there really won't be any complications?" the mother inquired in a worried, trembling voice.

"No, there won't," the doctor answered firmly, "none whatever."

This conversation must have reached the ears of the

sleeper. He lightly withdrew his hand from the doctor's grasp, stretched, and opened his eyes. Everyone came closer to the bed; even the bearded old man stood up and joined the rest.

Two restless, wondering eyes showed beneath the white bandages. The mouth was pursed in surprise, and then it uttered a soft, whispered query:

"What is it? Where am I?"

Before anyone was able to reply, Tom winced and closed his eyes. In that one single moment it all came back to him. He remembered the chase and the lake and the blows of the thick cane. He was sorry that he was not dead.

"Where is Father?" he asked, barely audibly.

"It isn't your father!" Koko spoke up suddenly, scratching himself behind the left ear. Then he noticed everyone looking at him. Seeing that, he added, "He's not your father."

"And Ivo isn't your brother either," Bozo continued, in a much surer tone of voice. It appeared as if he had known this for a long time; no one could have guessed that he had found it out from Tom's mother just a few minutes before.

"Mama," the lad in the bed said, slowly opening his eyes, "is it true?"

His mother knelt beside the bed and, trying to stifle her sobs, she whispered softly:

"It's true, Tommy. I should have told you before . . ."

Tom's eyes filled with a wondrous light. It was the light of gladness. What he had hoped for had come about. He knew that it was somehow impossible for his own brother and father to be thieves; yet it felt strange to realize that now he actually had no father or brother. He asked:

"And my real father? What about him?"

"He died, Sonny . . . a long time ago . . ."

"Mama, will you promise me something?" Tom suddenly asked, raising himself up slowly in bed and thus disturbing the doctor.

"I will, Tommy. Whatever you want!"

"Don't ever, ever cry again. There is no reason. From now on everything will be all right with us."

"No, I won't cry," the woman replied, standing up and wiping her tears on her apron. "Never again . . ."

This was not the only surprise that was to gladden Tom's heart that crisp sunny morning. First, the boys told how old Isaac with his blind dog and with Blacky's help had caught old Bran, and how both thieves were already in the hands of the militia.

"When I heard the shooting, I ran to you. I knew what was happening. Every night when I went to take my bath, I expected something of the sort." Here the old man fell silent for a while and then added, his toothless mouth grinning broadly, "I knew that you suspected me as well, devilish scamps, ha-ha . . ."

Then Bozo told how, when the war started, Mirko Bran had reported old Isaac to the authorities as a Jew in the hope of getting his wood saw. However, old Isaac hid in the forest beside the lake and saved himself.

Finally Emmie presented to the sick boy the camera that the poet had given to the boys as a gift. Cockroach had returned the camera to him that morning and explained everything. Mario had not even noticed that his precious apparatus was gone.

"If you sell it, you will have enough money to be able to spend about ten days at the seashore," the poet said.

"My father will pay for me," Cockroach volunteered, "so that it ought to be enough for three people. We shall go to some island and live like Robinson Crusoe."

"You meant to say that it will be enough for four," Bozo spoke up somewhat abashed. He hastily took off his glasses and began to blow on them. "I hope that we can take Blacky along."

"That's right," said Koko, turning to his friend in the

bed. "Blacky is awfully sorry. He asked you to let him visit you. He says . . ."

"Let him?" Tom interrupted him impatiently. "But I was never angry at him. Besides, you tell me that he helped me. Tell him to come right away. Go on, Koko, get him."

"By that time I will have coffee ready for all of us," said the woman of the house, going toward the door.

"Scrambled eggs for me," the sick boy shouted.

"Not on your life," the doctor spoke up merrily, happy to have an opportunity to say something at last. "Until you get well, you are not to eat any eggs or meat or cheese or . . ."

"All right, all right," Tom interrupted him, "but when I get well and when we go to the seashore, then I'll eat scrambled eggs every day. And meat and cheese and everything I am not allowed to eat now. And until then, until then . . . I'll eat only—when no one is looking!"

Everyone laughed except the doctor, who frowned. He was thinking how difficult and at the same time how easy it was with such young patients.